SHERLOCK HOLMES MYSTERY TALES

all new adventures!

by
Frank Thomas

2001
Gryphon Books
Brooklyn, New York
U.S.A.

SHERLOCK HOLMES:
MYSTERY TALES
by
Frank Thomas

Acknowledgements:

SHERLOCK HOLMES *MYSTERY TALES* by Frank Thomas contains 13 original stories and is copyright © 2001 by Frank Thomas. All Rights Reserved.

First Edition:
Gryphon Books: March, 2001

This is a Gryphon Books Original!

ISBN: 1-58250-036-3 $16.00

For additional copies of this book please send $16.00, plus $1.50 postage to:
**Gryphon Books
PO BOX 209
Brooklyn, NY 11228-0209
U.S.A.**

Send an SASE for a list of our great books and mags!

visit our web site at: ***www.gryphonbooks.com***

CONTENTS

THE SOFT FINGERS

It was a gray and overcast Sunday morning that found Holmes and myself up and about at an early hour for no particular reason. Diligent Mrs. Hudson, long used to our irregular schedule, had provided us with a hearty breakfast. I was seated by the fireplace going over some notes regarding Colonel Pendergast and the Tankerville Club scandal which I was thinking of making available to the reading public. Holmes, in his robe, was standing at his oft-used post beside the box window surveying the passing scene in the street below. Snow had fallen in profusion the night before. White flakes were not allowed to lie dormant on top of drifts but were seized by frequent gusts of wind and sent drumming against the glass of Baker Street windows. Holmes had just lit a cigarette when something caught his eye.

"Hello," he said, "I believe a message just arrived for us."

My intimate friend was not above pulling my leg on occasion and I attempted to return the compliment.

"Delivered, no doubt, by a former coal miner from Wales whose brother is now serving in Her Majesty's Navy."

Holmes chuckled as he crossed to the door of our suite of rooms.

"You mock me, my dear Watson. No, it is but a youthful employee of the telegraph office."

As the detective opened the door, I could hear the footfalls of our page boy on the stairs. Billy appeared at the entrace, silently handing Holmes a cable. The long thin fingers of the master sleuth extracted the message and his quick eyes darted over it.

"Thank you, Billy," he said. "No response. There will be a gentleman calling shortly and you can show him right up."

As Billy shut the door, Holmes crossed to the fireplace and handed me the message which I read aloud.

"Sherlock, I trust this finds you at home and that you will remain on the premises. A certain Mr. Wakefield Orloff will call on you shortly. I can vouch for his character and motives and trust that you can provide assistance through the use of your unique talents. In haste. Mycroft."

A tingle of excitement ran through me and I rose from my chair.

"This does sound interesting, Holmes. You were commenting just yesterday about the recent dearth of criminal cases."

"There is nothing to indicate that Orloff comes to me regarding a criminal matter."

"But your brother does mention your unique talents. I hardly think the gentleman wishes to discuss Australian wool production."

"Wakefield Orloff. Now I just wonder who he might be?"

As he wondered, my friend again regarded the street below and I joined him in his vigil. There were few passers-by and Holmes' eyes centered on a figure about a block away.

"I fancy that is our bird, Watson."

The man he indicated seemed short, with a bowler and a dark top coat. He was coming at a good rate, his feet automatically finding firm footing in the shifting snow.

"Note how he glanced at the house numbers," muttered Holmes.

As I nodded, a curious thing happened. The wind, which had relaxed into a temporary calm, suddenly revived with a violent gust. The man's bowler started to go with it and was, in fact, airborn for a moment. Then an arm shot out with amazing speed, snatching the hat brim and replacing it in one continuous movement. It was so fast that one did not quite believe it had happened. The man's stride had scarcely faltered during the split second action. My eyes must have widened and Holmes' breath came in with a soft hiss and then was expelled in a low whistle.

"Before the arrival of this emissary, I am taking the precaution of removing my revolver from the desk and placing it in my dressing gown pocket." Holmes did so.

"Do you feel this man could be an enemy?" I asked.

"Not with Mycroft's blessings. However, anyone with reflexes as fast as that has to be potentially dangerous. Let us trust that he is dangerous to others and not to us."

When our visitor reached the first landing of the stairs at 221 B Baker Street, he found the door ajar and entered. His eyes passed over the sitting room in a seemingly lazy glance that was not lazy and missed nothing. After the street incident just witnessed, I took pains to study him closely. The man was on the short side and seemed a little plump. It crossed my mind that what swelled his coat could be layers of muscle and not fat. His face was round and good humored with a mobile mouth. His dark hair was thin but arranged artistically and he had a small, well-brushed mustache. His clothes, not new, were well-cut. For a moment I thought he might be a retired army officer. Then I made note of his eyes which were very clear and a peculiar shade of green. I decided that, whatever he was, he wasn't retired. Yet there was nothing distinctive about him. Had I not been watching him like a hawk, I would have had trouble describing him at all.

He spoke in a low and pleasant voice. "Mr. Holmes, I am Wakefield Orloff."

"We have been awaiting your arrival. My friend, Dr. Watson."

"A pleasure, sir," said our visitor as he nodded to me. He then removed his hat which he carefully placed on the side table. A billfold appeared from an inner pocket and was flipped open. Orloff showed it to Holmes who nodded quickly.

"Some identification," I thought.

Orloff was out of his topcoat in a flowing motion and removed his gloves. Holmes made a half gesture towards the Queen Anne chair by the fireplace but the man chose the cane back beside the end table on which he had placed his bowler. He sat with his back straight and his weight balanced on the balls of his small feet. I wondered if he might have been a professional dancer at one time.

As Holmes took a chair, there was a moment of silence which the great detective broke.

"Do you know the contents of the cable I just received?"

"Only that it mentioned my coming here."

"I assume you know my brother?" Orloff nodded. "He requested that Watson and I be of what help we can."

As was his custom, Holmes had included me in the matter, something which Mycroft Holmes had not done. I made note that my friend had not mentioned who we were going to help and recalled that Mycroft had been vague on this point as well.

Orloff picked up the ball which Holmes had tossed his way.

"I work for the government-Foreign Trade Department-but that is not important. It was felt that the information which I bring would best be delivered in person. The situation relates to Sir Randolph Rapp."

"I know of the gentleman," stated Holmes.

"And therefore know that a great deal of important information passes through his hands," continued Orloff. "There is a definite indication of a leak. Certain moves of the government in the field of geopolitics have been anticipated. Pre-knowledge of these attitudes of Her Majesty's ministers could only be possible through someone in the Rapp apparatus."

"Because Rapp himself is so instrumental in forming these attitudes." Holmes seemed on familiar ground.

"Exactly," said Orloff. "Do you know Sir Randolph's work pattern?"

To my surprise, Holmes nodded. "His activities are centered around his home in Mayfair. Since he is not officially connected with any government branch, he visits various offices on occasion but uses his domicile as his headquarters."

Having never heard of Randolph Rapp, I almost interrupted with an obvious question but managed to preserve my silence.

"What is the composition of the Rapp household?" asked Holmes.

Orloff ticked them off. "Wife, Amanda Rapp. To be a part of her husband's work, she acts as a file clerk. Associate, Alexander Villers. Last living member of an ancient and famous family which came with the Norman Conquest. Considered a brilliant disciple of Sir Randolph. Butler, Ralph Cord. The other servants are not in residence. Government stenographers and office personnel with security clearance come to the dwelling when needed. Actually, I...it was felt that the fewer people living on the premises, the less chance of a leak. Unfortunately, this precaution was not enough."

Holmes was regarding his visitor keenly. "I assume that you feel the actual residents of the Rapp household are the only ones that could be involved in this security breach."

Orloff nodded. "Sir Randolph works in the fragile world of speculation. It is important for his efficiency to feel relaxed, without pressures or restraint. Villers is a working cog in the Rapp machine. He cross-checks information for Sir Randolph and studies official reports, principally from diplomatic sources. He also acts as a sounding board of Sir Randolph's occasional speculations as does Amanda Rapp. There is one other semi-resident, a Miss Hortense Frayne, Canadian, graduate of Ottawa University, Master's degree in psychology and sociology. Lives in a flat in Berkshire Mews but frequently stays over at the Rapp mansion. There is a bedroom permanently available for her there. She keeps an eye on the S.S. and C.I.D. Central Office reports. If there is a file on a particular person which catches her interest, or Villers' for that matter, it is brought to Sir Randolph's attention."

"Miss Frayne, then, can be included in the possible suspects," said Holmes thoughtfully, "unless..."

"Sir?" Orloff's expression was politely inquisitive. I noted that he had not moved a muscle since sitting down. With his hands folded in his lap, he had remained completely relaxed and motionless.

"Unless," continued Holmes, "Miss Frayne also reports elsewhere."

Evidentally, Wakefield Orloff had been given the green light by Mycroft Holmes. "A very clever investigator might conclude that Miss Frayne has an association with an intelligence organization, possibly in Canada or even here in Britain."

"So," said Holmes, "we have a wife, an assistant of impeccable credentials, another with friendly espionage connections, and a butler. We are to presume that Sir Randolph, himself, is above suspicion?"

"Undoubtedly," stated Orloff. "He has received high honors from his country and is extremely well-paid for his work. Upon retirement, not imminent I am happy to say, he will possibly write a sequel to his remarkable 'The Motivated Minds of Mankind.' He works with an absolute minimum of direction or interference. He is frank in declaring that the status quo is most satisfactory to him. As a guess, I would say the same applies to Lady Rapp."

Holmes' eyes flicked towards me briefly. I well knew that the great detective was recalling the amazing matter of the Right Honorable Trewlawney Hope. (see: "The Adventure of the Second Stain(1))

"Two points require answers," said Holmes. "First, a matter of procedure. Hypothetically, I am Villers, or even Miss Frayne. I bring a file on a certain person to Sir Randolph's attention. He feels the matter is of sufficient importance to demand his scrutiny and that his opinion should go to-say-the Secretary for European Affairs. What happens?"

Orloff's response was without hesitation. "Sir Randolph, after studying the matter, might write up an opinion immediately. He frequently does. Or he might send signals of inquiry or secure what information he needs himself. Whichever avenue he chooses, he prepares his final judgement alone. His conclusions are written in long hand while locked in his upstairs study. The material is then given by Sir Randolph to an official courier for delivery to-well, in the situation you present, Mr. Holmes, to the Secretary of European Affairs. The couriers have strict orders to take nothing from an intermediary. They receive Sir Randolph's findings from his hands only."

A smile of admiration touched Holmes' face. "A nice bit, that. The mark of the security expert."

If a gleam of satisfaction warmed Orloff's eyes, it was gone in a flash.

"Are there any exceptions to this procedure?" asked Holmes. Orloff nodded. "Frequently, Sir Randolph works late at night. Transportation of his findings would be hazardous and inconvenient. On those occasions he places his report in the safe in the living room. It is a Harley-Mills of the latest design. Only Sir Randolph knows the combination. And the combination is changed every month," he added with emphasis. After a short silence, Orloff continued. "You mentioned two points, Mr. Holmes."

"I can instigate certain lines of investigation now," said Holmes, "and I will. But the crux of the matter is meeting the quartet of potential suspects and viewing the Rapp mansion in Mayfair. I would be doing you and/or my brother an injustice if I did not conclude that you have a plan regarding that."

"I am just a messenger, Mr. Holmes."

It crossed my mind that he was a little too quick with this statement.

"However, we do have a stroke of luck," Orloff continued. "Sir Randolph has indicated a considerable interest in meeting with you relative to your recent voyage."

I had difficulty concealing my surprise at this statement. Holmes had, but recently, concluded a most sensitive case shrouded in secrecy because of its association with the King of Scandinavia.

A fleeting shadow crossed Holmes' face. "My journey to

Sweden was in connection with a very confidential matter," he said.

"To be sure," responded Orloff. "Also confidential is the Possibility that Her Majesty is considering a trip to that part of the world. Sir Randolph would greatly appreciate discussing the climate in that section with a trained mind."

"The political climate," said Holmes drily. He mused for a moment, then nodded as though in agreement. "What reason do we give for a visit to Mayfair other than the real one?"

"You do play whist, I believe."

"Watson and I have, from time to time."

"Excellent. Sir Randolph is quite taken by the game. With his wife, Villers and Miss Frayne present, you and Doctor Watson make a total of six. During the evening, it will be arranged that you and Sir Randolph are sitting out. At that time, you both could leave the foursome of players for a spot of brandy and a few words."

"A neat arrangement," said Holmes. "Do I detect some urgency relative to this matter?"

"You will receive an invitation from Sir Randolph for dinner and whist this evening," said Orloff.

Holmes had no more questions and Orloff had no further information to impart. So the matter stood. Our visitor departed to flash the "go" signal to Mycroft Holmes, no doubt. When the door closed behind Wakefield Orloff, Holmes sank back in his chair. With his elbows on its arms, his hands steepled and his nose touching their apex, the master illusionist of the mind sat gazing at the door in deep thought. Suddenly, he shook his head quickly and looked at me.

"Forgive me, Watson. We have had a tasty and interesting tidbit presented to us, have we not? And yet," continued the detective, "I find Orloff himself just as interesting."

"A messenger?" I assumed an expression of doubt but it was a sham. My naive question was no more than bait to see what rabbits Holmes might produce from the magician's hat that was his mind.

"Far more than that, Watson. Take the bowler which we saw him retrieve so quickly on the street and which he placed so carefully on the side table within easy reach."

"What about it?"

"The brim is reinforced with steel. In the powerful hands of Orloff, I am sure that it could be sent skimming through the air and deliver a stunning and perhaps fatal blow to whatever head it might come in contact with."

"Good heavens, Holmes! What a subtle and unexpected weapon."

"No more than the toes of his shoes which are steel-tipped. A kick to a kneecap would have a crippling effect."

Holmes' observations had me goggle-eyed. "What is the man-a walking arsenal?"

"Our departed guest is undoubtedly one of England's top security officers. Did you notice how his voice had a tinge of satisfaction when he mentioned that the safe combination was changed monthly? He slipped a little when he mentioned that the fewer people living on the Rapp premises the better. He started to say: 'I felt' and corrected himself to say: 'it was felt'."

"Now that you mention it, I do recall that. But, Holmes, who is this Randolph Rapp that you both seem so familiar with?"

Holmes' eyes assumed a dreamy look. "It is singular that a problem involving Sir Randolph should reach my ears. The gentleman owes his present position, in part at least, to my brother. As I have mentioned previously, Mycroft is the clearing-house for the opinions of every influential department at Whitehall. Only he can focus all the information into a tidy whole. It is Mycroft who equates how each factor will affect the other. The final conclusion, which often formulates governmental policy, is frequently the creature of Mycroft's meticulous mind. England, having done so well with him, decided to forge another tool. Policy may be decided by a government according to the whim of its rulers, but it is transmitted by men. All men have certain drives, certain factors which color their thinking and motivate their actions. Sir Randolph Rapp is an expert on the drives of men. He studies and then delivers an opinion as to how they will react under a given set of circumstances. He can deduce with uncanny accuracy whether a certain individual is dangerous to the state. I do not mean to imply that Sir Randolph is clairvoyant, but his record is singularly successful. His judgements of men have given England a definite one-upmanship in our foreign relations."

"Holmes," I exclaimed, "what an amazing situation!" "And one that can never be revealed." The sleuth took his cherry-wood from the pipe rack and crossed to the Persian slipper on the mantelpiece. "Oh, but the news media would have a merry time indeed revealing that the destiny of England is decided, in part, by the suppositions of a former Regius Professor of History at Cambridge. But it is what works that counts. Pragmatic England has a long history of losing battles but seldom a war."

With his pipe filled and lit to his satisfaction, Holmes instigated the lines of investigation which he had mentioned to Wakefield Orloff. Messages flowed from his pen to unknown destinations. Billy was kept busy with comings and goings and Holmes littered our sitting-room with his volumes of newspaper clippings. I kept silent and out of his way, well knowing that my friend was wandering through the labyrinth of his mind following threads of supposition, inference, and deduction anchored to the facts that he could unearth.

In the early afternoon, a special messenger arrived with the anticipated invitation to dinner from Sir Randolph Rapp. The distinguished author and scholar expressed his delight that we would be available. Directions were included and it was to be dinner at eight.

Holmes had been principally occupied with his newspaper files. Having, evidently, drained this source of information, he left Baker Street with an introspective air. I tried to rekindle my interest in the Tankerville Club notes but my mind kept wandering back to the strange-cloak-and-dagger affair we had become involved in. It was not until early evening that the detective returned. His manner had changed and he even hummed a bit of a tune as he hung up his greatcoat and deerstalker hat on the back of the entrance door.

"From your manner, Holmes, I sense that you have un-covered some valuable information."

"As to its value, I cannot say," responded Holmes, "but I have added to our general fund of knowledge. I learned from a former professor at Oxford that young Villers was a recluse. During his period at the University, he had no romantic entanglements and no friends for that matter. Actually, my learned friend was somewhat vague in recalling Villers. He did mention that he affected a beard during his college days to conceal his extreme youth. From other sources, I learned that Villers is now clean-shaven."

"But what possible value could that...?" I did not finish my question as a thought occurred. "Oh, I see what you're getting at."

"Please tell me, Watson. I don't see at all."

"You think this studious pose was a false front to cover some other activity."

"An interesting thought but facts don't bear it out. Villers was one of the most brilliant graduates in Oxford history. He studied, all right, and his marks proved it." As I registered disappointment, Holmes advanced another thought. "Relative to the butler, Ralph Cord, it might interest you to know that he was a long time member of the Villers household."

"Well, Holmes, that could indicate collusion."

"I don't know what it indicates, but these are things we can bear in mind tonight."

Holmes seemed prepared to drop the conversation and I quickly posed a question. "Did you learn anything about the Rapps or Hortense Frayne?"

"Didn't bother," responded my friend. "I rather imagine the capable Orloff knows everything important about them already."

That was all the information I was able to secure prior to our departure for dinner.

Night had long fallen when Holmes and I arrived at the

entrance to the Rapp estate. An impressive iron spike fence surrounded the rambling house and grounds. The gate was locked
but the gate house within was occupied by a big, broad-shoul-
dered, truculent-looking man who opened the outer portal when
Holmes provided identification. As we walked up the broad road-
way to the house, the sleuth indicated the watchman behind us.

"A loan from the Criminal Investigation Division, I'll
wager."

The lawns were close-cut and almost devoid of trees offering an open area between fence and mansion. Behind stout
wire close to the dwelling, I spied luminous eyes gazing at us.
Low and ominous growls eminated from that direction.

"Doberman Pinschers," stated Holmes. "They let them
loose when the household beds down for the night."

I shuddered. "Pity the poor swagman caught between
fence and house."

A massive front door was opened by the butler, who ushered us into a brightly-lit drawing room. The fort-like exterior
dissolved into a picture of comfortable English home life. My
feet sank into costly oriental rugs and I noted original art works
on the walls. As the butler retreated with our hats and coats, Sir
Randolph Rapp greeted us. I was surprised. The former professor, now motivational specialist, resembled a jolly toy-maker. His
face was ruddy and wreathed in smiles. His figure indicated a
sedentary life and his hair looked designed to defy a comb.

"Casualness seems the keynote here," I thought but I noted
that when Sir Randolph introduced his wife, he managed to have
Lady Rapp in the best light possible as she greeted us. Amanda
Rapp was quite tall with flaxen hair and a Dresden doll face. She
moved with the willowy grace that some English ladies seem
born with. It crossed my mind that she might be able to kick up
her heels if she wanted to. I had not forgotten Lady Hilda
Trelawney Hope who had become entangled in the web of the
international blackmailer, Eduardo Lucas.

Evidentally Lady Rapp was an avid reader. Over some
excellent sherry, she posed a number of questions relative to my

writings with particular emphasis on the Netherlands-Sumatra matter. It seemed strange that she would center on me with Sherlock Holmes present but I noted that Sir Randolph and Holmes were conversing by the fireplace in low tones. Possibly Sir Randolph was already discussing Her Majesty's proposed trip to Sweden with the sleuth and his wife was acting in concert with him by diverting me.

It was shortly before dinner that Alexander Villers and Hortense Frayne made their appearance. When the butler, Ralph Cord, materialized from the dining room with a significant glance at his mistress, and Lady Rapp gathered eyes and led the parade to the festal board, I resolved to study my fellow diners with the hope of presenting a shrewd observation to Holmes.

Over a sumptuous repast, Holmes fielded some queries that his fellow diners batted his way relative to the Mazarin stone affair and then Sir Randolph deftly led the conversation around to the international situation. To spare Holmes embarrassment no doubt. This gave me time to consider the others at the long oaken table. Alexander Villers was meticulously dressed and had a wiry, well-put-together body. From the neck down, he looked like a fencer. But his head was that of a scholar and his face was dominated by large, almost myopic, brown eyes. Smiling did not come easily to him but his manner was affable enough. Hortense Frayne, from Ottawa, was small and quite dark. Her movements were quick and nervous and her figure was underslung with a long waist and rather short legs.

"She doesn't look like an espionage agent," I thought, "but then what espionage agent does?" I wondered what a spy was supposed to look like and didn't come up with an answer. My attention returned to the conversation.

"We are an unfortunate number for whist," Sir Randolph was saying.

"We shall play cut-in, Randolph." It was Lady Rapp speaking.

"That way, we can all play with Mr. Holmes," Hortense Frayne colored slightly and added, in haste: "...and Doctor

Watson, of course."

"Wants to be able to tell her friends that she played cards with the great detective," I thought. Then I had another idea. "The wily fox is going to study their reactions at the table. Sir Randolph may just be motivating himself onto a slide of Sherlock Holmes' mental microscope."

After coffee, we gathered in the drawing room where the butler, Cord, had arranged a card table and chairs. Holmes spread a deck for the draw but, with a movement singularly clumsy for him, managed to allow a number of cards to spill over the side of the table and onto the floor. The alert butler retrieved the pasteboards and Holmes secured them from his hand. An expression akin to alarm flashed through the servant's eyes but Holmes seemed embarrassed and the look faded to be replaced with the impassive visage, seemingly a trademark of that particular and unique species known as "the perfect English butler."

The luck of the draw found Holmes paired with Hortense Frayne against Villers and Sir Randolph. It was Villers' deal and I noted for the first time that the third and fifth fingers of his right hand were deformed. However, he dealt the cards easily enough and play began with Lady Amanda and myself as spectators.

The players seemed capable enough to my inexperienced eye. Holmes, of course, knew what he was doing. He had read several books on the game by Alexander Deschapelles, considered the greatest whist player in the history of the game. After a short period, my eyelids grew heavy and I had to prod myself to keep awake.

Then Sir Randolph and Holmes were out, replaced by Lady Amanda and myself. As my friend conferred with the former professor over brandy, I tried to do my best at the card table. I don't really know if I succeeded or not.

Finally the evening came to an end and Holmes and I departed from this most unusual household. Walking towards the gate, I was thankful that the Doberman Pinschers had not been released for their nightly patrol. As the burly watchman closed the gate behind us, a carr iage drew up. I recognized the

battered topper of the cabby. It was Phinease Portney, Holmes' favorite driver. The sleuth had him on a monthly retainer,
As soon as we were seated, the carriage assumed motion and, without a directive, headed for Baker Street.

"Did you learn anything, Holmes?" I asked eagerly.

"As much as I could hope to. What about you, old friend? Any conclusions?"

Possibly my response surprised Holmes for I had been going over the entire matter during our dull evening at cards.

"I may be in error, Holmes, but I have formed an opinion."

"Excellent! Where does your finger of guilt point?"

"When we return to our chambers, I will write down my prime suspect and put the name in an envelope. Then, after you have worked your cerebral magic, we shall see if our theories agree."

For some reason, this suggestion seemed to tickle Holmes.

"Capital, Watson! It shall be so. But, and this in no way interferes with your idea, did you make note of anything during the whist game?"

"Everyone seemed capable enough. Possibly Hortense Frayne was over cautious. Making the right move did not seem as important to her as not making the wrong one."

"An excellent analysis with which I concur."

"How does she fit into this picture, Holmes? Wakefield Orloff as much as told us that she is a member of British Intelligence."

"As is common in matters of this kind, there is a watchdog within the house as well as the Doberman Pinschers outside."

"I see. Miss Frayne."

"I'm sure she is well-qualified for her duties. She would have to be, working with Sir Randolph. But her prime function is to provide a pair of watchful eyes within to augment those without." Holmes mused for a moment and then continued.
"Did you have any thoughts regarding Alexander Villers?"

"He was the best player of the lot, Holmes. Too bad about the chap's fingers."

"Deformity in the hands is an hereditary defect of the Villers family. They date back a long way, you know. Unless Alexander has an heir, the family dies with him."

One of the most remarkable characteristics of Holmes was his ability to turn his brain off like a water faucet when he felt he could no longer work to advantage. The remainder of our return trip to Baker Street was spent in conversation unrelated to the case at hand.

I was surprised to find our sitting room unoccupied when we returned. "Here now," I said, "I expected Orloff to be waiting for us."

A tight smile creased Holmes' face as he lit the oil lamp on our desk and the flickering light threw strange shadows on his hawk-like visage. "True to his instincts, the singular Mr. Wakefield Orloff has faded into the background. But I would hazard a guess that we have not seen the last of him." (Any readers of my words relative to the world's greatest detective know that Holmes' guess was dead center. Orloff was involved in many cases following this one.)

Our page boy had a number of messages that had arrived during our absence and Holmes went over this harvest that his communiques of the day had reaped. One large package produced an impressive pile of clippings which he selected for study. As he progressed, I noted that he tossed most of the neatly clipped newspaper columns aside, though he did retain several which he placed under the seashell by his right hand. The seashell, used as a paper weight and ash tray, was from the island of Uffa where Holmes and I had almost perished.

Rousing himself from a thoughtful moment, Holmes indicated the printed matter.

"Carruthers of the Standard has been most helpful. But I do wish he would train his reporters differently." My blank stare spurred him to continue. "Young newspapermen are told to consider a story from five angles:

Who? What? Where? When? Why? For our purposes, I wish they would add the word, 'How?'"

"I am not following you, Holmes."

"How did people look? How did they react?" Holmes picked up another clipping. "It must have occurred to you, Watson, that in most of the matters that come to our attention, we are cast in the role of the 'Johnny-come-lately'. Other hands have fingered the evidence. Other minds have already considered the facts. We must look where they have not. The little things."

Holmes' eyes became riveted on the clipping in his hand. "He's indicating a considerable amount of interest in that one column," I thought.

As though reading my mind, Holmes spoke again: "Now here is something. The account of a famous wedding. 'The bride wore blue to match her dancing eyes.'" Holmes read for a moment and then quoted again. "'The groom was in the traditional family kilts but looked very Irish with his raven black hair and piercing blue eyes." The detective mused over the clipping for a long moment, then tossed it on the desk top. He swept the others back into the envelope in which they had come. "Watson, would you be good enough to hand me that box over there?" He indicated a cardboard container which he used from time to time as a repository for certain news items. "I say, old boy, have you jotted down your suspect?" he asked as I brought him the box.

"I shall right now," I answered and I did so.

Holmes was considering the contents of the cardboard box. "There are some rare birds here, Watson. Criminals of note who have been out of circulation for some time."

"Incarcerated?" I asked.

"No. Just missing."

There was a discreet knock on the door which then opened to allow Mycroft Holmes to enter. The second most powerful man in England had carte blanche regarding access to our chambers.

"I thought you might drop by," said his brother.

Favoring me with a nod, our visitor lowered his unwieldy

frame into the Queen Anne chair and fastened his alert, steel-gray eyes on the younger Holmes.

"An annoying business, Sherlock," he said. "Have you arrived at any conclusions?"

"I have. So has Watson."

"Are you in agreement?"

"We shall soon know. Let me present a compendium of the matter." The sleuth began pacing the room slowly, pausing from time to time to make a point.

"Regarding this security leak which could seriously affect affairs of state, we got off to a good start. The idea of using the game of whist as an excuse for our dining with Sir Randolph was excellent. More relative to that later. I was puzzled by the outline of the situation presented by your security agent, Wakefield Orloff."

"I didn't call him a security agent," said Mycroft Holmes.

"You didn't have to." The sleuth's tone was dry. "Orloff gave us five suspects, if we include Sir Randolph. Then he promptly narrowed the field to two, pointing out that Sir Randolph and Lady Amanda lacked motive and Hortense Frayne was actually an agent of the government. I began to wonder why my astute brother had bothered to involve me in the case at all. The process of elimination gave us a good prima facie case against Alexander Villers. I was diverted from Villers momentarily but had to come back to him because of the card game which provided an immediate inconsistency. Alexander Villers was a scholar from early youth and, like others of the type, was withdrawn from the world. His Oxford professors described him as a 'loner.' How was it that this introvert was such a good card player? The game of whist requires people, something that Alexander Villers had shunned."

"That is an angle that we never considered." Mycroft Holmes' placid manner was, for the moment, abandoned.

His brother became very brisk. "When I first learned of this puzzling affair, a gnat began buzzing around my head in an irritating fashion. Obviously, Mycroft, you had done a great deal of thinking on this matter. Obviously, Alexander Villers was your prime suspect. Why had you not done something about it?"

The elder Holmes' face became stern. "Sherlock, one just doesn't go around accusing the last member of one of England's oldest families without conclusive proof. There was also the problem of how Villers secured his information. He has ready access to portions of Sir Randolph's work but not the summations."

"How about Cord?"

Mycroft Holmes shook his head in irritation. "The butler leads to another frustrating dead end. Ralph Cord, prior to his position with Sir Randolph, spent his entire life in the service of the Villers. He was the only one of the servants in the Villers Castle in Northumberland who really knew Alexander. He went to work for Sir Randolph on Alexander's recommendation. What would transform this perfect butler into an agent for a foreign power? More important, what talents would he have that would make him of any value to an espionage ring? It is an endless circle, Sherlock."

"Until you step away from it and regard it from a different angle." Sherlock Holmes had that cat-like look that I had seen before. "I wondered if you knew about the butler."

"We knew a lot of things," stated the intelligence chief in a bitter tone. "But nothing seemed to help us."

"Perhaps this will. Tonight I chanced upon something which definitely implicated Ralph Cord. I was forced to conclude that Cord is not the man we think he is. It was but a short step to the conclusion that the same situation could exist with Villers. Having gotten that far, I needed a theory as to what had actually happened and the proof. The theory was easy and I just found the proof before you arrived, Mycroft."

Holmes had positioned himself by the hearth fire, one arm resting on the mantle piece. It was a pose that he fancied at moments like this.

"Consider, if you will, this unique situation. We have a young heir who spent much of his childhood and early manhood away at schools. After his graduation from Oxford, with a smashing scholastic record, his parents had an unfortunate accident. Their carriage horses bolted and both perished when the vehicle crashed. To try to recover from shock, Villers took an extended trip to Europe. Now, these are all facts but when you put them together, an unusual picture emerges. In elite circles, everyone knows of Alexander Villers but, with the death of his parents, nobody really knew him. Somewhere in a far off office or embassy there was someone sufficiently perceptive to realize that young Villers presented a golden opportunity. My theory was that he went to the continent but never came back."

A realization was born in Mycroft Holmes' eyes. "I could not accept him as a traitor. An imposter is another thing."

"The masquerader," continued Sherlock Holmes," was undoubtedly selected because of a strong resemblance. Everything possible was done to augment this. It must have taken a fine surgeon indeed to duplicate the deformed fingers of the right hand which were an hereditary mark of the family. Fortunately for the scheme, Villers affected a beard at the university. Now he is clean-shaven."

I could restrain myself no longer. "Holmes, what makes you so certain of all this?"

"My dear Watson, I just read you an old clipping relative to a famous wedding. It was the nuptuals of Alexander Villers' father and mother. The reporter made note of the fact that both the bride and groom were blue-eyed. But the imposter has brown eyes." Holmes glanced at his brother. "The name of Gregor Mendel may mean little to you, Mycroft, but it will undoubtedly ring a bell with Watson here."

"The founder of genetics," I exclaimed.(2)

"Exactly," said the sleuth. "The Mendelian Law proves that two blue-eyed persons cannot have a brown-eyed offspring. Therefore, the man we know as Villers must be an imposter."

"But the information?" His brother was persistent on this point.

"For shame, Mycroft. You know the security measures at the Rapp household are extensive. The information can only come from the safe where Sir Randolph's opinions are frequently placed prior to their being handed to a government courier."

Mycroft Holmes started to speak, but his brother cut in quickly.

"I know what is bothering you-the deformed fingers. The imposter is right-handed and with only three working digits he could not 'crack a crib,' to use the vernacular of the light-fingered gentry. But you are forgetting the butler. I rather imagine that if your capable Wakefield Orloff takes a trip to Northumberland, he will find the true Ralph Cord still living there. No one bothered to check this possibility. Everyone took Villers' word regarding the man's identity. But I find that the present butler in the Rapp mansion fits the description of one Cosmo Tracy. You may not know of Tracy but the Nottingham Bank people do, along with others. Cosmo Tracy is a master cracksman and I believe it is he who opens the Rapp safe when the pseudo Villers gives the word."

I was regarding my friend with amazement, not altogether prompted by his revelations.

"Whatever alerted you to the butler?" asked Mycroft Holmes.

"During dinner this evening I noticed something. Later I was able to confirm my suspicions. I managed to let some cards drop from the table prior to our game of whist. The butler retrieved them for me. In taking them, I was able to feel the tips of the fingers of his right hand. They had been sandpapered. It is an old trick. Increases the sensitivity of the fingers to the fall of the tumblers. An American safe-cracker, the greatest of them all, originated the technique. His name is Jimmie Valentine."

Mycroft Holmes slapped his knee explosively. "By George, we've got them."

"But let us not take them," replied his brother. "You and your associate, Orloff, have the makings of a coup here, Mycroft. It will take doing but if the reports that go into that safe are carefully doctored, I rather imagine the employers of the false Villers and his cracksman cohort will get hopelessly confused."

There was a satisfied expression on the massive face of the older Holmes as he rose to his feet indicating that, in his mind, the case was a fait accompli. However, his brother detained him.

"We still have Watson's suspect to consider," he stated with a twinkle in his eye.

I was ready for this and silently handed Holmes my envelope with, I hope, an unrevealing expression. Extracting the sheet of paper, my friend read aloud: "Ralph Cord." His eyes widened in surprise which dissolved into admiration. "Watson, you solved it. The supposed Villers pushed the button but the butler did the deed. Here I have been combing newspaper files and delving into family history and you produce the culprit like a slight of hand expert. What thread led you to unravel this tangled web?"

I chose my words with care. "You might say I went with the tide."

"I fail to follow your ratiocination," said Mycroft Holmes.

"No matter," I continued, with an attempt at an off-hand manner. "Ever since I became your brother's chronicler and made certain of his exploits available to the public, there has been a rash of stories dealing with mystery, mayhem and murder. Completely fictitious, of course, but they all have one fact in common. In every story, it is the butler who did it."

Sherlock Holmes smiled. "A distinct touch, my dear Watson. A distinct touch indeed."

THE IVORY ELEPHANT

There was an ominous overcast to the sky when Sherlock Holmes and I found our way to the Cafe Royale where we ordered an early supper. This was the night of the monthly meeting of the Marleybone Swing Circle, an event which did not warrant a squib in the Daily Telegraph or Star but was dear to our landlady's heart. My intimate friend had informed Mrs. Hudson that we would not require her considerable talents with stove and skillet this evening, an arrangement which allowed her to leave early for her social gathering.

I fretted somewhat during our meal being in haste to return to our chambers. During those final years of the last decade of the nineteenth century, Holmes' schedule was awesome. He was consulted on every case of notoriety of that period and the newsprint headlines could have served as his work calendar. Since the journals of late had been much devoted to the theft of the famous emerald of the Countess of Chilton, I had been anticipating a visit from Lestrade or Hopkins or Gregsori perhaps, relative to the filching of the famous gem. No message greeted our return so I settled down in our sitting room with my fellow tenant in anticipation of a quiet time at home. The wind had come up in the early evening with ever increasing force and now was howling down Baker Street, driving the attendant rain fiercely against our windows. Laying aside the latest copy of "The Lancet," I rose to beat flame from the logs on the grate and then crossed to a window to view the deserted thoroughfare. Street lamps gleamed on the rain washed pavement and a solitary carriage was splashing from the Oxford Street end.

"Not a fit night for man nor beast," commented Holmes, his head rising from the Evening Standard.

"Agreed," I said, "nor for an investigation far..."

Then I cut my words short for over the wail of the wind there was the sound of horse's hooves and the rasp of an iron shod wheel as it ground against the curb. The carriage which I had seen was now stationary before our door.

"Who can this be?" I said, somewhat aghast, for it was no night for social calls.

"A case, old fellow, and I judge some person in dire distress. Do tend to the outer door for we do our own greeting this evening."

It must he relative to the Chilton emerald, I thought, as I made my way down the seventeen steps from our first floor landing. But when the light of the hall lamp revealed our visitor, I abandoned this thought. No police inspector this, but a comely young lady. As I escorted her back up the stairs, I made note that her carriage remained at the curb. This provoked an inward groan for surely she was bent on taking us out into the storm, probably to a distant section of Mayfair.

Our fair visitor informed me that she was Geraldine Connor and hoped that she might intrude on Mr. Sherlock Holmes. When I made introductions in our chambers, Holmes greeted her with that easy courtesy for which he was remarkable. Helping with her coat, I escorted Miss Connor to the laburnum Queen Anne chair. Her straight, Stewart red gown was of the latest fashion girdled just under the bosom. She wore a broad-brimmed hat tilted somewhat in a Duchess of Devonshire fashion, over one ear. Holmes, standing with his back to the fire, watched her with interest as she seated herself, revealing shapely ankles in the process. I shared my friend's interest.

"You can speak as freely before Doctor Watson as before myself, Miss Connor," he said by way of relieving a potentially awkward moment.

The woman, I should say girl, folded her hands in her lap

attempting to adopt a business-like manner but there was a nervous air about her. She accepted Holmes' statment without demur.

"Gentlemen, I fear I have been indiscreet."

"So say we all at one time or another." Holmes had much experience in getting clients started on their tale of woe.

"I know of your wonderful reputation, Mr. Holmes, and have read Doctor Watson's recountings of your adventures. Consequently, I rehearsed how I would present my problem to you but..."

"...it still comes hard," said Holmes, seating himself in the cane back with his customary grace.

"It can be told briefly though it may not be a matter you will find interesting. Commonplace, I fear." A moue of distaste crossed her aristocratic features. "I am to be married to a young man of good family. Prior to our engagement.. .before we even met...I knew someone else rather well. There were some letters..."

Her delicate face colored and she turned from us to the fireplace as though from shame. I made note of her splendid profile. A deep breath caused her bosom to rise and fall deliciously and then she continued, forcing the words out.

"Certain sentiments which I expressed on paper were compromising. The...err...gentleman approached me regarding them and I paid him a considerable sum for their return."

Holmes shook his head in a negative fashion. "He did not give the letters back.."

"Oh, he did, Mr. Holmes. I secreted them away in a private hiding place of mine, inside an ivory elephant from Siam. Two nights ago the elephant was stolen."

Drat it, I thought, was there ever a woman who would destroy love letters?

"Who is this former.. .friend...Miss Connor?"

"Lester Snavely. He owns a curio shop on Godolphin Square."

"I know of the establishment," said my friend. "Am I right in assuming that you suspect Snavely of stealing the ivory elephant and the letters concealed inside?"

The girl nodded. "I received a note from him. On the surface an innocuous message stating that he had quoted me a price too low on a certain object in his shop and would be glad to discuss the matter further. I knew what he meant, of course."

"I'm still surprised that he returned the letters."

"At the time I bought them, I don't believe Snavely knew of my pending marriage. My fiancee is high placed, Mr. Holmes."

"I understand. What would you have me do?"

Geraldine Connor shot a quick glance in my direction, then returned her intense gaze to Holmes. "The elephant and the letters are my property. Perhaps this is woman's reasoning, but I see no crime if they are returned to me. Should I go to the police..." Her delicate hands fluttered in a helpless fashion... "it would all come out. Snavely would see to that."

I could not supress a question? "Miss Connor, are you proposing that we steal the ivory elephant?"

"Merely return it to me, Doctor Watson."

"That does have a better ring to it," said Holmes, darting a quick glance at me which silenced the rejoinder on my lips. "Where is the elephant?"

"In Snavely's house on Sackville Street."

"It might be hidden elsewhere."

"What need? Snavely expects me to pay. I might have but for reading Doctor Watson's account of one of your cases involving a blackmailer. Did you not use the words, 'bleed the victim dry' Doctor?"

My heart went out to this poor girl and I was much heartened by Holmes' next words.

"We shall certainly look into this matter, Miss Connor. Can you tell us anything about Snavely's place of residence?"

"He lives in a small Georgian house. I shall give you the address. A maid and gardener come in the afternoons and are not in residence. I suspect his principle income is blackmail and he does not wish servants around save when he is at his shop."

Holmes nodded. "Snavely obviously knew of the secret

compartment in the ivory elephant. Might he not have taken the
letters from it and disposed of the piece?"

The girl rejected this. "Lester...Mr. Snavely...is greedy.
The elephant is of some value and he will certainly keep it. Besides, I'm convinced that he anticipates no problem regarding
this matter."

"That is all we need to know." Holmes rose indicating
the meeting was over. "I shall contact you when..."

"Please, Mr. Holmes, could I come here? I'm frightfully
upset by this matter and would prefer..."

Holmes did not let her unfinished request hang in the air.
"Of course. Would tomorrow noon be convenient?"

"I am most grateful," said the girl, rising.

After I had escorted her to the waiting carriage, I bolted
back upstairs to confront my friend.

"Did you make note of the vehicle that brought our visitor, Watson?" asked Holmes as I closed the door to the landing
behind me. He was standing by the window gazing at the street.

"Not especially."

"Pity. I thought I detected a crest on its door but a flickering street lamp does not provide the best illumination."
"A crest?"

"Then there was that medallion on the choke collar around
her neck."

Since I regarded him blankly, he continued, somewhat
dryly.

"Perhaps your eye was drawn to a slightly lower level.
The medallion carried the arms of a noble family, the Briants."

"Then you think her name is not Geraldine Connor?"

"Rather certain of it."

"Holmes, this becomes a matter of great social importance. A titled marriage no doubt. What do you intend to do?"

"Secure the ivory elephant."

"In the daytime?"

"The larcenous art of burglary is most often practiced
under the blanket of night but I know of nothing in the criminal

code which makes it more illegal if done by day."

I crossed to gaze for a moment at the embers of the fire and then turned to my friend suddenly.

"Holmes, as you know, I'm a bit of a stickler for propriety but I heartily endorse your decision. Rather a matter of chivalry, you know."

"Coupled with the fact that our visitor read your case history of the Charles Augustus Milverton matter," replied Holmes with a chuckle.

I bristled a bit at this. "It might have been the 'Second Stain' affair," I replied defensively.

"Touche," said Holmes and that was all I could get out of him regarding this singular incident.

The following morning I slept later than I had intended. When I descended to our sitting room, the smell of Holmes' shag was everywhere but he was not. This sent a momentary chill through me but surely he would not embark on such a hazardous matter alone. Mrs. Hudson said that he had departed without leaving a message and consoled my anxiety with basted eggs and some rashers of bacon. I was on my second cup of coffee when, much to my relief, Holmes entered our chambers.

"You've been scouting the lay of the land."

"I've been scouting," he replied, "prompted by a small squib in yesterday's Standard. The shop of Lester Snavely was entered night before last. The police have a suspect in custody, one Philip Drazin, who has a record as a jewel thief. The case is complicated by the fact that Drazin had no stolen goods on his person."

"Good heavens, Holmes, you knew all this yesterday? Doesn't it cast a different light on Miss Connor's story?"

"Not quite so, Watson. We suspect the lady's name is not Connor and it is possible she did not tell us all. Why was she so certain that the ivory elephant was in Snavely's home?"

"She instigated the nightime entry into his shop," I exclaimed with sudden understanding.

"I'll buy that in part, good fellow."

The other questions bubbling on my lips were interrupted by the arrival of Billy, the page boy. He had a package which he handed to the sleuth.

"Just arrived, Mr. 'Olmes. 'Twas the thin man."

I knew what that meant. As Billy departed, I exploded. "Slim Gilligan, the cracksman. You had him secure the elephant from Snavely's house."

"Watson, you have, indeed, developed the ratiocinating mind," said Holmes as he opened the package. He set a gleaming object upon the surface of the desk and I hastened to inspect it. Ivory, all right, of a white almost translucent color.
"Nice piece."

"I'd say so." Holmes' long, thin fingers fiddled with the elephant and then there was a click and a piece of the figure's bottom came loose. Reaching into the revealed aperture, Holmes removed a packet of letters. Standing close by him, I realized the paper was perfumed.

"Well then, it's all done," I stated with a despondent air. "Old friend, you shock me. I almost believe you regret not having been part of a surreptitious and illegal entry."

Since Holmes had struck right at the truth, I returned to my morning coffee in something of a huff. He replaced the letters in their hiding place and busied himself with his Common Place book. I resolved not to ask him more regarding the matter but await the appearance of our client.

She finally arrived, a bit earlier than twelve. Though the rain and wind of the previous evening had passed on, her face still held a dewy freshness. In the light of day, I was able to confirm the fact that she was a singularly attractive and well formed lady.

No sooner had she entered our sitting room than she spied the elephant on the desk top.

"Oh, Mr. Holmes, you've secured it." She was regarding him as though he had just helped preserve the Empire, something he had done and would do again.

With a gesture of modesty, ill suited to my friend, he stepped aside and indicated the ivory object. "Best make sure your letters are within it, Miss Connor."

With trembling fingers, she did just that, leafing through the packet of perfumed missives eagerly.

"They're all here," she said with relief and then almost ran to the fireplace into which she threw the pages eagerly. As she watched them turn to ash, a look of peace came over her statuesque features.

"At last, the sword of Damocles is removed," she said, almost to herself. As she returned to the desk to secure the ivory elephant, there was a suggestion of moisture in her luminous eyes.

"Mr. Holmes, you have done me a great service."

The sleuth had crossed to the door which he opened, signalling down the stair well. I assumed he was alerting Billy to get a hansom for the lady. Geraldine Connor made as though to depart but a gesture from Holmes halted her.

"A moment. The ivory elephant is yours but there is something else within that is not." Her face was suddenly frozen but she did not resist as he secured the object from her. This time Holmes fiddled with the head and, after a moment, it came loose in his hand. The door behind us revealed, of a sudden, the wiry form of our friend from Scotland Yard.

"Ah, there you are, Lestrade," said Holmes with his thin smile of triumph. "Let me introduce you to Slick Sally Wills who is the wife of Philip Drazin."

I was stunned by this revelation and then even more amazed at the burst of green fire in Holmes' hand. From the head of the ivory figure, he had extracted a six-sided stone of startling brilliance and it glistened in his palm.

"And here, Lestrade, is the emerald of the Countess of Chilton. Guard it with care and I'd keep a close watch on Slick Sally as well."

When the door closed on a gleeful Inspector and his prisoner, I whirled to face my friend. "All right, how did you know?"

"The Chilton emerald was stolen on the continent and a

number of suspects were rounded up including Philip Drazin but there was no trace of the famous gem. Drazin and his wife, who works with him, wished to get the stone back to England for the call of the hills of home is heard by thieves as well as virtuous folk. Besides, the market for gems is better here at the moment. They concealed the emerald in a shipment of ivory objects consigned to Lester Snavely who deals in such things."

"He being one of the gang."

"Not so. Fellow doesn't know a thing about it. When the jewel thief and Slick Sally returned to our shores, Dazin burgiared Snavely's shop, intending to secure the gem and leave the ivory elephant, of course. But a problem arose. Evidentaly Snavely was intrigued by the art object and took it to his home. Dazin was apprehended and is still being held by the police so Slick Sally decided to have us secure the ivory elephant for her."

"I still ask, Holmes, what put you on to this scheme?"

"You have made note, in your writings, that I am more than a bit choosy regarding the cases I accept. To sweeten the bait, Slick Sally tried to give the impression of being a titled lady by wearing a medallion bearing the arms of nobility."

"And placing the same crest on the carriage that brought her," I said, nodding with understanding.

"She picked the wrong crest, old boy. The Briants, historically, were violently opposed to the Bonnie Prince Charlie revolt. No female of that ancient and illustrious family would be caught dead in a dress of Stewart red. Once I became suspicious of our client, the true reason for her interest in the ivory elephant was not too hard to find."

"And the letters?"

"Flim flammery in anticipation of possible complications. It was a case not without a number of interesting points, Watson. You might make mention of it sometime in your writings."

And I have.

THE INSIDE STRAIGHT

It was a mild evening in early spring. After one of Mrs. Hudson's top drawer dinners, Holmes and I took a hansom to Wynn-Chichester's book store off the Strand. The sleuth had Wynn-Chichester on the alert for any publications dealing with a Frenchman of the past century, one Alexander Deschapelles. The career of this soldier, who had lost an arm fighting for the Corsican, interested Holmes. Despite his injury, Deschapelles achieved fame as a billards champion and was described as the finest whist player the world had ever seen. I knew there was something else about the Frenchman that had intrigued Holmes. My friend distrusted chess players and Deschapelles, having studied the game for a mere three days, had not only challenged the champion chess player of the world but had beaten him.

Wynn-Chichester, whose business dealt mainly with specialized books, assured Holmes that he was on the trail of a volume with information about Deschapelles and the sleuth and I then took a stroll on the Strand before returning home.

We were greeted at the door of 221 B. Baker Street by an anxious Billy, the page boy, who took the detection business seriously.

"Elderly gent waitin' fer you in sittin' room, Mr. 'Olmes. Come 'round 'bout an hour ago," he added, taking our coats. "I tol' him you'd return 'bout this time." Billy's voice dropped to a confidential level.

"'e's a client, Mr. 'Olmes. Mark me words."

"If you say so, Billy. Our schedule is unusually clear at the moment. I knew that I could depend upon you."

Holmes made for the stairs leaving behind him a wide eyed, worshipful lad with a purpose that the oceans of the world would never turn.

"One day," I thought, mounting our seventeen steps in the wake of the sleuth, "Inspectors Lestrade, Hopkins and even Alec MacDonald will be forced to the wall by destiny's tot." If Billy didn't end up at least Superintendent of Police, I would lose a monstrous wager with myself.

There was the scent of strong tobacco in the air as we entered our chambers. A white haired figure rose from the Queen Anne chair, a smoking cigar in one hand. I recognized it as the East Indian variety that Holmes fancied during this period.

"Mr. Holmes," exclaimed the stranger, "and surely Doctor Watson. The boy said to make myself comfortable and I did." He waved the cigar expressively. "Hope you don't mind?"

"Not at all," replied the sleuth. "Surprising that you located them." Holmes' choice of the coal-scuttle as a humidor was not standard procedure, even in America. I knew that was our visitor's point of origin from his speech.

"Name's Bill Boehiert, gentlemen, and I'd be grateful for a little of your time."

The sleuth gestured assent while lighting a cigarette and positioning himself by the mantle. Billy, having hung our coats on the hooks behind the hall door, withdrew with a curious glance at the stranger as though in search of clues.

I tried to do the same as I seated myself on the sofa. Our visitor's hair and lined face indicated age but he had risen on our entrance with a spryness that belied it. His voice was strong.

"Findin' the ceegars was no trick." A gnarled index finger tapped his prominent proboscis. "The nose told me. Ain't lost me sense of smell. Leastways if it's bacon fryin' or a fire in the grate on a cold mornin' or a ceegar." He savored a puff. "This here's a good 'un."

"East Indian," replied Holmes.

"Do tell?" Keen blue eyes, deepset in a bony face, surveyed the sleuth shrewdly. Holmes' manner had been somewhat brusque.

"Don't know if my problem is of interest to you or not, sir, so let's have at it."

Extracting a single piece of parchment-like paper from his coat pocket, Mr. Boehlert passed it to the great detective. "Hmmrn. Bearer bond for one thousand American dollars. Issued by the Union-Stuyvasant Bank of Syracuse, New York." Holmes fingered the paper and then surveyed it with his ever present pocket glass. "What about it?"

"That's what I come to you fer, Mr. Holmes. Is it the McCoy?"

"You have some reason to be suspicious about its authenticity?"

"Wouldn't have 'cept fer somethin' which was said."

"We'd best go at this from the beginning, had we not?"

"Right you are, Mr. Holmes."

With a resigned look as though forced to accept the fact that this matter would take a little time, Holmes shot a suggestive glance at the Tantalus but Boehlert declined my offer of a drink as he plunged into his story. Holmes indicated no interest either so I poured myself a tot of brandy, though, in retrospect, I feel it unseemly to drink alone.

"I'm a newcomer to these shores, sir. Mining's my business but I sold out a couple of years back and fer a good price. Poker's my passion and that's paid the freight as well. Decided to see a bit of the world which seems the fashion with us Americans these days. The years go by and we want to mosey 'round where our roots once was. I come over here on the 'Olympiad' a week ago. Don't know no one here but I got a nice layout at the Trinity Hotel and looked 'round fer a little action. Museums and the like not being exactly my cup of tea. Anyways, I fiddled around

a bit with that Chemin der Fer game and the wheel, 'bout breakin'
even, till I found me three gents who played poker. Leastways,
that's what they said. So we got a nice quiet little game goin' and
I done all right. On the last hand of the night, it got down to me
and this limey..."

Boehlert came to a jarring halt and swallowed hard.

"Beg pardon, I mean this here gent who had fallen in love
with three aces. I'd drawn to an inside straight and filled it. Nobody noticed that the gent didn't have enough on the table when
he finally called me so we was facin' a little problem. But he
produced that there bond with the statement that it was as good
as cash which seemed on the up and up to me. He was in to me
fer a hundred and fifty of your pounds so I give him two hundred
and fifty bucks, American, and the game broke up."

As Boehlert's words flowed forth, Holmes' manner mellowed and there were tell-tales of interest about him and even a
twinkle of humor at the man's faux pas.

"You said..." he began.

"That somethin' made me uneasy 'bout this here bond.
Dunn' the game there was small talk, like always, and it was
mentioned that California Jim had recently come over here to
England."

Holmes crossed from the mantle and seated himself in
the chair by the hearth fire. He was interested now.

"California Jim Anderson?" he asked, as though already
knowing the answer.

Noting that the name struck no chord with me, Holmes
explained.

"If talent were the only measure of an individual, Mr.
Anderson would be a treasured American possession. He's the
finest forger the States have produced."

"You can see what come to my mind after the game broke
up, Mr. Holmes," continued our visitor. "Here's an obvious En-
glishman with a bearer bond from a bank in the States. With California Jim on the scene, the bond might be a bit of his handiwork
that he brought along with him."

Holmes had made his decision. "All right, Mr. Boehlert, I'll learn whether this property of yours is authentic or not. I'll have to keep it, of course, so best I give you a receipt."

"No need, sir," stated Boehiert promptly. "Even Stateside we know about Mr. Sherlock Holmes."

Surprisingly, the sleuth seemed flattered and slightly embarrassed at this gesture of confidence.

"What casino was the site of this high stakes game?"

"Don't reckon I mentioned it happenin' in a gambling hall."

Holmes' lips twitched with humor. "Mr. Boehiert, in England, or America as well, Chemin der Fer and Roulette are not parlor games."

A loud guffaw burst from our client. "Got me there, all right. No cockleburrs under your blanket, Mr. Holmes. Do you know of a place called The Nonpareil Club?"

Now it was I who guffawed and even Holmes could not restrain a smile.

"Did I say somethin' funny?"

"It's a long story, Mr. Boehlert. Let's just say we do know of the Nonpareil." (see **Sherlock Holmes and the Golden Bird**.)

"Fancy layout. The owner was real interested in poker..."

"One moment," interrupted the sleuth with as much genuine surprise as I had ever seen him show. "Do I understand that you played poker with Baron Dowson?"

"That was his handle, Mr. Holmes. Then there was another titled gent..."

"Count Negretto Sylvius."

"Fer a fact. You do know all about this here Nonpareil Club."

"And you took them both for, I believe the expression is, 'a bundle?'"

"Wasn't too hard, Mr. Holmes, poker hem' somethin' of an American game. It was the third gent, Wells, who was the heaviest loser."

"Mr. Wells I do not know. In poker, it is my understanding that three of a kind is a good hand."

"Yep. Not good enough to beat an inside straight though."

"If your Mr. Wells was anything like his two friends, you certainly drew three of a kind for table mates. Baron Dowson heads up the most organized gang of criminals in London and Sylvius is his right hand man. The Nonpareil Club is their headquarters and the fact that you relieved those scoundrels of some of their ill gotten gains gives me intense pleasure."

"Well bless my soul and bottom."

"I beg your pardon," I interjected, trying to follow the man's colorful way of expressing himself though, for all I knew, in his native habitat his words might have been commonplace indeed.

"Sorry, Doctor Watson. I mean...well I don't know exactly what I mean. That's just an expression we use."

"Do I deduce that you will be visiting the Nonpareil Club again?" asked Holmes.

"Tomorrow night."

"By then I will get word to you regarding the bearer bond. If it is spurious, you can demand its face value in currency. If not, you can accept others of the like as payment. I am very interested in your winning just as much as you can."

"Me, too," said our client rising from his chair. As he retrieved his coat and hat, his right eyelid lowered in a slow wink. "If it will set yer mind at ease, those gents may be hard cases but they don't play poker so good." On this heartening note, he departed.

Holmes was rubbing his hands together in a most satisfied manner.

"We have a tasty tidbit on our dish, do we not, Watson?"

"It would seem that fate has given you a tool to wreck vengence on the Baron Dowson group."

"There's more to it than that. What, at first, seemed a minor matter now warrants calling out the troops."

"Good heavens, Holmes! Slim Gilligan and Company?"

"Indeed. To borrow from our client, the nose tells me. It is going to be a busy night but I shall not require your invaluable assistance during the opening moves so you might as well..."

"Hold on," I interrupted with some firmness. "You are not going to toddle me off to bed with my mind awhirl. What about this famous or infamous California Jim, the forger?"

"If he is in England, and I believe he is for the grapevine of the lawless is remarkably accurate, there is nothing to arrest him for. Nor will the Americans institute extradition proceedings. They might have caught him for his last escapade but fate took a hand."

Realizing that my intense interest would not be denied, Holmes elaborated.

"About a year ago, a hitherto unknown letter from Lord Nelson to Lady Hamilton surfaced. It caused a sensation and fetched a large sum at an auction at Park-Benet. No less an authority than the late Sir Nathan Gildersleeve authenticated it."

"The famous handwriting expert," I exclaimed, much surprised. "Surely it wasn't a forgery."

"California Jim's work. But if the case goes to court, Sir Nathan cannot appear to reverse his opinion or, he was a crusty old devil, to stand behind it. The only result would be a blemish on the otherwise flawless record of a dead man. As a curio, the letter is now worth more than was originally paid for it so there is no one to swear out a complaint."

"How did they discover that it was forged?"

"Pure happenstance, Watson. The son of the man who bought the letter was a chemistry...I suppose 'freak' is as good a word as any. He discovered fragments of a wood fibre that was not used in the manufacture of paper during Lord Nelson's time. But for that, the letter would now be considered genuine and a somewhat colorful insight into Lord Nelson's life would be history. What do you think of that?"

"I think California Jim is good."

"You might repeat that several times on your way to bed."

I did.

The following day was a bustle of activity on Holmes' part which all came together in the evening. In one respect, the entire affair was pure delight with excitement and suspense as its running mates. However, my participation was sheer lunacy and I felt like the greatest fool alive standing in the main gambling room of the Nonpareil Club with a turban on my head, a profusion of erzatz whiskers and my skin dyed a dark brown. On my third finger sparkled a blue sapphire, on loan to Holmes from Runnels and Bridges, the jewelers who were greatly in the sleuth's debt. As Holmes had applied the finishing touches to my makeup and the costume which came from his seemingly limitless wardrobe of strange apparel, I had to admit that none of my fellow practitioners on Harley Street would have dreamed that this seeming Indian Maharajah was naught but good old Watson. I summoned every objection that I could but my friend told me I never had to say a word. Just an aimless gesture touching my forehead and lips would impart the suggestion that I was under a vow of silence and any further interest in me would be devoted to the flawless stone on my finger. Of course he was right.

So I wandered around the lavishly furnished room regarding the various games of chance with, hopefully, wise eyes as though I were, at any moment, going to sit down and take a run at the bank.

Finally, what I had been alerted for happened. There was a sound of chairs scraping from Baron Dowson's office at the head of the main stairway at one end of the room. Then two of Dawson's men who were guarding the office were jostled aside as the door opened suddenly and our client, Bill Boehlert, appeared brandishing a Frontier Colt revolver. With practiced efficiency he wacked the wrist of one of the guards with the long barrel of his weapon and my medically trained ears heard a snap of bone. Then the muzzle of the colt jabbed the Adams apple of the second guard and he was rolling on the floor, clawing at his throat as I made for the outer portal according to instructions. Down the stairs came Boehlert showing excellent speed for his age and behind him was a bewhiskered waiter whom I did not

know but the walking stick in his hands was an old friend. I recognized it as Holmes' sword cane. As Count Sylvius rushed down
the stairs followed by Dowson who was tugging at his hip pocket,
there was that chilling sound of slithering steel and Sylvius came
to a jarring halt, sheer terror in his eyes. Small wonder for the
needle sharp end of two feet of Toledo steel drew a thin line of
blood from the dimple in his chin and then hovered suggestively
in the vicinity of his throat.

By then I had brushed past the doorman and stood at the
entrance of the gambling club. Across the street, Burlington Bertie
and his brother Tiny had apparently been loading kegs of beer
onto a wagon but actually waiting for my turban to show. With a
rush they were at the entrance. A casual shove from Tiny sent the
muscular doorman rolling head over heels down the steps, across
the sidewalk and into the gutter. Then the brothers were inside as
a carriage drew up with Slim Gilligan in the Box. I entered it
followed shortly by Boehlert and the waiter whom I now realized was Holmes. From inside the club came a crash of sound
and a body came hurtling through one of the windows carrying
the drapery with it. Burlington Bertie and Tiny, who had demolished a veritable army of assassins in a back alley in Cairo
(Sherlock Holmes and the Sacred Sword) were at it again. There
were the dull thuds of bone colliding with flesh and another body
flew out the door followed by a staggering man intent on going
elsewhere, anywhere, quickly. Then Slim whipped up the bay
gelding and the closed carriage assumed motion as Bertie and
Tiny also came out of the considerably demolished Nonpareil
Club. Trotting beside the carriage they effortlessly pulled themselves to the roof behind the driver's seat. I detected creaks of
protest from the body of the vehicle when Tiny's weight was
added to the cargo. As we careened down the street, I peered
through the small rear window at a scene of wild confusion.
Dowson stood at the entryway yelling for reinforcements while
mopping blood from a swollen nose. The urbane Count Sylvius
was hanging onto the door with one hand while the other clutched
his stomach as though in fear it was not there, his body in a half-

crouch of pain. A third figure that fitted the description of Wells bolted from the club without a word to his damaged cohorts. As he hastened down the street, a shadow moved in a nearby doorway and a small form seemed to glide after him.

"So that's it," I thought. "Slippery Styles, the human shadow." When Holmes wanted someone followed, Styles was the man he called for. My friend contended that Slippery could follow a sinner into Hell without getting his coat singed. Things began to take shape for it was obvious that Holmes' agile finger was stirring more than one pot. Aside from temporarily putting the Nonpareil Club out of business and denting the financial resources of Baron Dowson and Company, he wanted to know where the mysterious Wells with his American Bearer Bonds resided. At least that was my analysis of the situation at the time and fancy my surprise when I learned that I was right.

Having caught his breath and slipped his awesome piece of artillery into his belt, Bill Boehlert was regarding Holmes with wonderment.

"You chaps do things in a big way. What happened?" Holmes was chuckling as he removed his disguise.

"You did your part so it was my duty to see that you were allowed to leave the premises with your winnings.   Dowson, Wells and Sylvius thought they had chanced upon a prize mark with money burning in his pockets but you rewrote their somewhat obvious plot line and an artistic job it was."

"Oh shaw," murmured the American, "like I said, poker just wasn't their game."

"When they realized that fact, they were obviously not going to take a considerable loss standing still hence the beginning of a rough house. Having insinuated myself into the premises in the guise of a waiter and with Watson to alert the rescue squad, our escape was no great problem. I noted that you won two more of those American bonds."

"Right here, Mr. Holmes," said Boehlert, handing them to my friend, not without a touch of pride I might add. "Excellent. Does Dowson or any of his people know where you are staying?"

Boehlert shook his head. "Didn't see no reason to bring that up."

"We shall play it safe in any case. The two lads will keep your suite under observation for the night," said Holmes, with a gesture towards the roof of the carriage.

"You mean them two one-man armies? I don't have a worry in the world."

"Bertie and Tiny are quite effective," admitted the sleuth. "Friends of mine, you see."

"Mr. Holmes, you've got some real unusual friends."

"And I'm always on the lookout for more." Holmes was regarding the American keenly. "With specialized talent, of course."

Boehlert's manner was half puzzled, half apprehensive as the carriage delivered him and his two bodyguards for the night at the Trinity Hotel.

Two hours later, back at Baker Street, a message had arrived from Slippery Styles and Slim Gilligan had been dispatched for points unknown. As Holmes stuffed shag into his Cherrywood, I felt that I had suppressed my wheelbarrow load of questions as long as I could. One can go just so far in catering to the whims of the world's only consulting detective and certainly the most eccentric one. Again, I was surprised when Holmes chose to discuss the matter.

"It was the bonds, you see. Quite genuine by the way but I knew that from the start."

With an effort, I remained silent, not wishing to interrupt Holmes' revelations.

"Wells, a man who patronized the Nonpareil Club and knew Baron Dowson and Sylvius, did not fit the part of a banker or financier who would use the readily negotiable bonds to formulate, or consumate for that matter, a monotary arrangement. Since I did not know of him, it was reasonable to assume that he operated on the Continent or in America. A cable to Inspector Johanets Schmitz of the Berlin Police instigated a search of the

Meldwesen files, that exhaustive body of information of criminal matters created by the machine-like logic of the German mind. We were rewarded. Wells is a thief who works the trans-Atlantic liners. I already knew that one Hubert Fatheringill, Vice President of the Union-Stuyvasant Bank of Syracuse, New York was on the Olympiad which arrived last week. During the trip over he was robbed of two hundred thousand dollars worth of bearer bonds issued by his bank. The matter has not been made public for a variety of reasons."

I could hold back no longer. "Our client, Boehlert, was on the same liner."

"Whether he knew about the theft or not is immaterial. One of the stolen bonds surfaced in the poker game and set this chain of events into motion for which we must be grateful to Mr. Boehlert."

"You had Styles shadow this Wells fellow and now you've sent Slim Gilligan to steal the bonds back."

"Set a thief," quoted Holmes with a smile. "I imagine Slim will have little trouble since I told him where to look."

I could well agree with my friend. Before deciding to cast his lot with Sherlock Holmes, Gilligan had been the finest cracksman of his time. Then Holmes' last remark registered on my poor, befuddled brain.

"Do you mean you know where Wells has the bonds hidden? Good heavens, how?"

"Wells is a shipboard thief, old chap. Hiding something in as confined a space as a cabin is difficult indeed. Crooks of Wells' type generally open one of the small portholes in their cabin and affix their loot, whatever it might be, to the outside of the ship where no one would even think to look. That's the tip I gave Slim tonight and we shall see if I was right."

He was.

It was mid-morning of the following day that Bill Boehlert joined us at Baker Street, eager to learn what final disposition Holmes had made of the matter. When the sleuth told him of the shipboard robbery he seemed thunderstruck.

"Holy cow! Two hundred thousand smackers?"

"Which I have here," stated Holmes, indicating a packet on his desk. "Or I will have when I add the three bonds you won in the poker game and that brings up an interesting point." The sleuth rose to knock out the ashes from his cherrywood into the fireplace.

"The money you won from Dowson, Sylvius and Wells has no bearing on this case, but the three thousand dollars in bonds does, However, I've arranged a solution which I think you will find satisfactory. The Syracuse bank is insured by Inter-Ocean, an organization for which I have performed some services. Inter-Ocean is prepared to pay the standard ten percent for the return of the bonds and no questions asked."

"Twenty thousand bucks!" The American could not supress a low whistle.

"You unearthed the bonds and I found them so I propose that we share the reward, ten thousand American dollars apiece. How does that strike you?"

"Right where I live, Mr. Holmes. You've got a deal. But what about the thief, Wells?"

"I wanted to get this matter settled before I loosen Scotland Yard on Wells. Possibly we can tie Dowson into the matter but I doubt it."

Boehlert had risen to his feet and was vigorously shaking Holmes'.

"One added proviso," said the sleuth and I noted that the American's enthusiasm dwindled somewhat.

"I have a feeling you may be staying in England for some time. I wonder if you'd keep in touch. There just might be some other activities that you could play a part in. Things of a specialized nature, of course."

Holmes and Boehlert were standing, their eyes locked and the silence continued so long that I began to feel embarrassed. Then the American shrugged.

"If you say so, Mr. Holmes. Back home I think we'd say that you are in the driver's seat."

Leaning against the mantle, Holmes was looking singularly smug as our visitor's footsteps dwindled down our stairs.

"What was that all about?" I asked, somewhat indignantly, for I had that sinking feeling that there was an entire chapter of this matter of which I was not aware.

"My dear Watson, you are a stranger in a strange land and wish to know if you have been hoodwinked by a counterfeit bond. Where would you go?"

"Why...to a bank," I stammered, this thought never having occurred to me.

"Yet Boehlert came to me? Why? Because the world's greatest forger doesn't want to be asking about a counterfeit anything in a bank. Our client is none other than California Jim Anderson."

"You mean, we've been dealing with a criminal."

"There's no charge against him, Watson, on either side of the Atlantic. I believe he's smart enough to keep it that way. Anderson, himself, stated that I had some unusual friends and the time may come when we'll need the services of the world's greatest forger. Certainly my brother, Mycroft, could in those cat and mouse games he plays in international espionage."

Holmes exhibited a very satisfied smile as he lit up his cherry-wood.

"I think that we've not only completed a financially satisfactory case but we may have added to our group of very specialized associates."

"I think you're drawing to an inside straight."

"Touche, my dear Watson."

THE DOUBLE DECEPTION

It was a warm, sunlit day in early summer. During the morning I had made some patient calls while Holmes had tidied up his volumnious files. He had but recently brought three cases to a successful conclusion but there was nothing in his manner to indicate depression or boredom which so frequently beset him when his superb brain was not busy solving some intricate puzzle or forestalling a nefarious scheme. He seemed quite jolly upon my return from morning calls and suggested a stroll along the Strand following lunch. Somehow people seem to picture Holmes as spending the major portion of his time in our untidy flat on Baker Street clad in a silken robe and smoking furiously or, when he braved the outer world, always wearing a deerstalker cap and an inverness. Such was not the case at all. The deerstalker and inverness were his costume when we made some lengthy trip and he frequently took constitutionals and was a bit of a dandy when he did so. My friend was recognized as one of the finest amateur boxers in England and was a single stick champion and he kept himself fit. A good thing it was, considering his usual schedule of activities.

Sherlock Holmes and I had no sooner returned to our chambers at 221B Baker Street than activity beckoned with an insistent and intriguing finger. The great sleuth was in the process of donning his purple dressing gown when there was a gentle knock on our outer portal.

"Come in, Billy," he said. Though I had noted nothing, his uncanny hearing must have detected a footfall on the seventeen steps leading upwards to our first floor and, in keeping with his frequent statement that a step can be as identifiable as a face, Holmes had anticipated a familiar presence.

Upon entering, our Page Boy silently handed Holmes a business card.

"By all means have him come up," said Holmes turning to me and adding, by way of explanation, "Poindexter. Do you know him?"

"I fear not."

"Works for Trans-Ocean Trust. Insurance division."

I well recalled the banking firm that my companion made reference to. It was the matter of The Treasure Train that Holmes handled for them so brilliantly that came immediately to mind. I had not realized that this financial institution boasted an insurance arm and was about to make mention of this when our visitor appeared.

Mr. Poindexter was a little man with side-whiskers. He wore a pince-nez perched somewhat precariously on the end of his nose which, possibly, contributed to the nasal quality of his voice. Though a mite Dickensonian appearance, there was a shrewd look about him.

"Mr. Holmes, forgive my arrival without prior notice, but my mission is so pressing that I rushed over in hopes that you would be available."

"My colleague, Doctor Watson, and I just returned, so possibly fate is well disposed towards this meeting. Do sit down," added Holmes, indicating the basket chair but a short distance from the desk.

Poindexter must have had dealings with the world's only consulting detective before. He indicated no surprise when Holmes secured shag from the toe of the Persian Slipper on the mantle with which to fuel the brier he fancied on occasion. Declining my offer of a libation, the insurance man plunged into his story with a rapidity that I knew would weigh well with Holmes.

"Are you, sir, familiar with the Sunburst Topaz?"

"By reputation. I have never seen the piece nor, to my

knowledge, has it ever been in this country."

"It is now," replied Poindexter with a suggestion of distaste. "I could wish otherwise. Runnels and Bridges, the jewelers, arranged to purchase it. Payment to be made upon delivery to England. The Topaz was in the possession of the somewhat wayward Prince of the ruling house of Carpathia. Matter is complicated by the fact that leading English insurance companies, Trans-Ocean included, have barred several European countries as regards comprehensive policies against theft.

"Runnels and Bridges insured the item with my company. The phrasing of the agreement is: 'Insurance to be in effect upon arrival in England of the Sunburst Topaz.' I approved the contract, assuming that arrival in England would mean the delivery of the stone to Runnels and Bridges. Such proved not to be the case."

"What actually did happen? There has been no note of an incident in the journals." Holmes' manner was soothing. Poindexter's pince-nez had been wobbling during his. recounting of the preliminaries and had finally fallen off as he referred to his personal involvement.

"The matter is but two hours old," replied the insurance man. "Guy Spaull, a man of some reputation on the continent, was selected as the courier to deliver the stone."

"The man is known to me," said Holmes. His manner did not reveal how. "Bit of a soldier of fortune. Not exactly the type for a job of this kind."

"I fear Trans-Ocean was somewhat casual about that," admitted Poindexter. "Our...my feeling was should there be any folderol on the other side of the channel, we would not be involved.

"But the incident occurred here," was Holmes' sage assumption.

"Spaull went to the Metropole from Victoria and deposited a box containing the Topaz in the hotel safe. He then contacted Runnels and Bridges, requesting that someone be sent to take possession of the piece."

"Why did he not just deliver it to the jewelers?" I asked

instinctively.

"He pleaded fear of being waylaid. Claimed that there had been an attempt to enter his compartment on the train de luxe from Cologne and felt that he was followed whilst on the Calais-Paris Express. He was much relieved to arrive at the Metrople with his cargo intact and decided to wash his hands of the responsibility at that point."

"Such an attitude is not unreasonable," commented Holmes. "If it was known that he was carrying the Topaz..."

Again my curiosity prompted an interjection. "But Topaz is semi-precious."

"Not this piece," replied Poindexter with a sour look. "It is the finest quality golden Topaz of the type mined in the Urals. The Runnels and Bridges policy is for twenty thousand pounds, which was the purchase price, by the way."

"Good heavens," I exclaimed. "A piece of mineral worth that much?"

"Not a large piece either," said Poindexter. "As you know, Doctor, Topaz is a hard, transparent substance, a compound of aluminum, silica, and fluorine. The golden variety is the precious type being a species of yellow sapphire. The sunburst has an absolutely unique color, almost a radiance, hence its name."

"You stated that Spaull deposited the Topaz in the hotel safe at the Metropole," said Holmes, bringing us back to the incident of the moment.

"Runnels himself hastened to the hotel and I tagged along. We conferred with Spaull in the dining room. He described his trip, at some length I thought, and handed the papers relative to the purchase to Runnels. We then went to the hotel desk. The clerk, much to our astonishment, stated that Mr. Spaull had already requested the Topaz and had signed a slip for its removal which is the practice at the Metropole. Of course, this story did not hold water since Spaull had been with Runnels and myself. Under questioning, the clerk admitted there had been one peculiar occurrence. When withdrawing the Topaz, the pseudo Spaull removed his glasses and the clerk noted a mole under his right eye which he did not recall having seen before."

"Guy Spaull having no such mole," said Holmes.

"Correct. The impersonation involved a masterful disguise, for Spaull was known to the clerk. However, that helps us not one whit. The Topaz is gone and I fear that Trans-Ocean faces a bit of a problem."

"I wonder," said Holmes softly, his eyes opaque with thought. "Let me wager that Spaull, on behalf of the Prince of Carpathia, is requesting payment for the object. His argument being that he fulfilled his obligation by delivering the piece to a place of security in London. How do Runnels and Bridges stand on the matter?"

'They seem prepared to pay the agreed price, figuring to be reimbursed by Trans-Ocean."

"Have you considered having it rumored about that you would be willing to ransom the Topaz? Such arrangements have been made in the past relative to incidents of this kind."

Poindexter's chin jutted out in a pugnacious manner, not in keeping with his general appearance.

"I, for one, would strongly object to such a move. Dealing with the criminal makes one, morally, a co-conspirator and while it might cut losses on one claim, I feel it would lead to future problems without end."

"Well, Mr. Poindexter, you take a very ethical position indeed." Holmes' tone was dry. "Naught remains but to have some words with participants and see what information we can dredge relative to this bizarre occurrence."

We did just that but not in the manner of previous cases. Holmes, to my delight, deputized me to assume an active role in the investigation. Delivering me by Hansom to the Metropole, he requested that I interview the desk clerk and suggested that I have some words with the staff of the hotel dining room as well. Then he departed for a Downing Street address with no explanation regarding the matter that claimed his attention elsewhere.

My duties involved the sifting of familiar facts. The clerk was cooperative, repeating a number of times that he had been so certain that it was Guy Spaull himself who had claimed the stone. I learned again that the impersonator had removed his glasses to sign the claim slip, at which point the clerk had noted the mole which was unfamiliar to him. The chap berated himself for not having become suspicious at this point. I comforted him as best I could, as is the habit of members of the medical profession, and made my way to the dining room.

The waiter who had served Spaull, Runnels, and Poindexter, was a German named Voss. He made mention that the three men had spent some forty-five minutes at a corner table and that he had served them coffee and pastry during their conference. He added, regretfully, that his arm had been inadvertently jostled while pouring a cup of coffee, some of which had spilled on Spaull's trousers, but the gentlemen had made light of the matter and retired briefly to the men's room to remove the stain. Upon returning, he made no further mention of the accident. In a conspiratorial manner, Voss added that Mr. Spaull had left him a sizeable tip.

Armed with this knowledge, which seemed of no import, I made my way back to 221B Baker Street, but Holmes did not return till sometime later. Then he patiently listened while I made my report in, I trust, a business-like manner.

"My good Watson," he said with a wry grimace, "I fear you fell into a trap. But we all must learn, and experience is the finest teacher. Having had the matter outlined by Poindexter, you sought but to confirm words."

I regarded the sleuth blankly. "Could you elaborate on that?"

"What new information did you glean from your questioning?"

He rather had me there until I thought for a moment.

"I don't recall Poindexter mentioning the spilled coffee." My tone was somewhat defensive.

"Agreed. That information is not without interest. Possibly you learned more than you realize. Let us backtrack. Guy Spaull came to the Metropole from Victoria Station. Did he deposit the packet in the strongbox before going to his room or after?"

"Before."

"Then what did he do?"

"Retired to his room. To freshen up, I assume, and to contact the jeweler, Runnels."

"Possibly Poindexter as well. Then?"

"He returned to the lobby and conversed with the desk clerk waiting for the gentlemen to arrive."

"Where did he meet them? In the lobby? In the dining room? Or do you know?"

"As a matter of fact, I do," I replied with a touch of asperity. "After a time, Spaull went out on the sidewalk, waiting for the arrival of Runnels and Poindexter's carriage. I verified that with the doorman."

"They returned to the lobby together?"

"No. They went to the dining room through the street entrance. After their conference they approached the desk via the lobby door leading to the dining room."

"Ah, then there are two entrances to the dining room. Now did you have their table pointed out to you?"

"I did. Table for four."

"Didn't inquire regarding that, I assume?"

"I certainly did. Mr. Runnels expected an additional arrival." I consulted my notes feverishly. "By happenstance, the waiter knew the gentleman. Here it is. Edwin Lister."

A beatific expression stole over Holmes' face.

"Perhaps, Watson, I can retire and raise bees sooner than I anticipated, leaving the disposition of the criminal classes in your capable hands."

"But when Lister arrived the Topaz had already been stolen. Is he important?"

"Possibly. Happens to be the first-rate authority on famous gems. Let us consider. We have Runnels, Poindexter, and Guy Spaull in the dining room with Edwin Lister due to arrive. At this point a man disguised as Spaull comes to the desk. Did he enter from the street?"

"The clerk really didn't know. He looked up from his duties and the chap was there requesting the packet from the strongbox."

"Hmmm, a dead end. But you inquired, which is important. Then there is the vital information you secured which puts the whole matter in its proper perspective."

'What, pray tell, was that?" My manner was resigned. I had seen Holmes embark on one of his summations before. The devilish thing about them was that he was always right.

"The imposter requested the packet from the hotel safe. On signing the receipt for it, he removed his glasses."

As I regarded Holmes with inquisitive eyes, a suspicion began to flutter, moth-like, on the periphery of my mind.

"If one wears glasses," continued Holmes, "one would normally use them to sign a paper, not remove them. That point is highlighted when we consider that, but one thing prevented the imposter's disguise from being perfect."

"The mole under his eye," I exclaimed automatically.

"Exactly. Yet he took pains to expose this blemish, to reveal his Achilles Heel to the desk clerk."

"What do you deduce from that?"

"There was no imposter and it was important to plant the seed of suspicion in the mind of the desk clerk so that it would bear fruit later."

Holmes was exhibiting that self-satisfied air that I frequently found grating. Now, seemingly, he shifted to nonsequiturs.

"Our metropolitan dailies have made mention that the Prince of Carpathia, reputed to be a bit of a wastrel, recently broke the Bank at Monte Carlo."

"Good for him," was my instant retort, having a fondness for the gaming tables myself. "But with such a windfall, why would he sell the Topaz?"

"Why indeed? The society columns inform us that the Prince is attempting to reinstate himself in the good graces of his family."

"Sowed his wild oats, eh?"

"It would seem so. His mother, titular head of the royal house of Carpathia, was born in November."

A shadow of irritation must have crossed my face and Holmes chuckled. "Patience, ol' friend. Let us link these items into a chain of conjecture. Were you the Prince, suddenly affluent from a gambler's lucky streak, would you not consider a gift to your mother? Said gift being the Sunburst Topaz? Topaz is the birthstone of November, remember."

"You mean as a gesture of reconciliation."

"The idea seemed so obvious that I made use of the diplomatic cable to uncover, through privileged sources, the fact that the Sunburst Topaz is, at this moment, in the vaults of 'Demler and Sons' prominent jewelers of Vienna who are affixing it in a setting as a surprise gift to the Queen Mother of Carpathia."

"Then it's never been in England at all!"

"Nor did the Prince consider selling it to Runnels and Bridges. The entire scheme was handled via telegraphy with no meeting of the principals."

"Why now it is as plain as a pikestaff," I chortled. "Spaull brought naught from the continent but a dummy box. Absenting himself from the dining room, he entered the hotel through the lobby door and requested his parcel from the strongbox. In effect he impersonated an impersonator."

Holmes was regarding me with seeming delight. "You are doing splendidly, ol' chap. Pray continue."

"Spaull returned to the dining room, detouring to the men's room to flush away the parcel and the bogus mole he had used to lay a false scent."

"Better and better."

Encouraged by his manner, I plunged ahead. "Now he plans to secure the twenty thousand pound sale price and disappear before his swindle is uncovered."

"I could split hairs about your phrasing, Watson, but all told, your reconstruction is accurate."

"We have merely to lay our hands on Spaull and the affair is all wrapped up." I was quite delighted at having solved the matter using, naturally, the analytical reasoning from effects to causes which my intimate friend had made famous.

It was early evening when Holmes told me the bad news.

"I sent a message to Lestrade regarding the Topaz matter. Alas, our obtuse Inspector-friend descended on the Metropole with much sound and fury. Spaull caught wind of his peril and slipped away through the tradesman's entrance. He is, at the moment, at large."

I gave vent to an expletive but Holmes seemed unconcerned.

"We'll lay the dashing soldier of fortune by the heels one of these days. In truth, it is not Guy Spaull that I'm concerned about."

I regarded him with a slack jaw. "Who then?"

"His cohort in this elaborate deceit. The whole matter of the Sunburst Topaz was very loosely arranged. There had to be someone on the spot to grease the wheels."

"But a while ago I had this solved." I could not suppress the tone of anguish in my voice.

"In part... in part. Now consider certain inconsistencies. The jeweler, Runnels, might well have insisted on payment on delivery at his place of business. Someone persuaded him to act otherwise. The wording of the insurance policy did not touch all wickets as is the practice of such documents. Again the indication of a machiavellian influence. Lastly, the removal of the fake package from the hotel strongbox was too rushed, too subject to mischance to be a planned action. It was a spur-of-the-moment improvisation, and Spaull thought fast, I'll give him that. Up to a point, all went well for the conspirators. The meeting in the dining room was to conclude with Spaull giving Runnels the package supposedly containing the valuable gem stone. Runnels and Poindexter were to depart and, at some predetermined place, their Hansom was to be waylaid and the package stolen. But Runnels upset the scheme by requesting Edwin Lister, authority on gems, to drop over to the Metropole and authenticate the Topaz there. When this unforseen arrangement was revealed,

Spaull moved swiftly to get rid of the packet before Lister arrived. He managed to jostle the waiter, Voss, causing the spilling of the coffee. In the confusion, a wetted finger found its way to the sugar bowl. You will recall, Watson, that Poindexter's pince-nez gave every indication of falling off while he was here."

"And finally did."

"Small wonder. One of the rubber grippers attached to the nose piece had been removed. That was what Spaull used as the bogus mole, affixing it under his eye with wet sugar which possesses a certain adhesive quality."

"Strange Poindexter didn't notice what had happened."

"But he did."

"He's involved, then?"

"Up to his neck. But with Spaull at large, I have no way of implicating Poindexter. Not a shred of proof to tie him into the matter. Therefore, Mr. Poindexter will be entered into our 'Future File'."

Holmes thought for a moment, then a smile tugged at his lips. "Of course, the minute Poindexter outlined the matter, I knew there was flim-flammery afoot. Consider, Watson, we were expected to believe that someone could disguise themselves perfectly as to pass as Guy Spaull without question. There is only one man in the world who could have effected such a masquerade."

I could see where this was leading us but my friend had earned his moment. Trying to preserve an innocent expression, I contributed my expected *leit motif* question.

"Only one man in the world? Who might that be?"

"Sherlock Holmes," was his bland reply. He was never one to consider modesty as a virtue.

THE DORCAS ALIBI

An early winter snow had fallen on London, covering the great metropolis with a thin blanket of pristine white. The frigid cold that had plagued us for the past week was, as it so often is, relieved somewhat by the frozen particles that fell like lazy confetti from an overcast sky. The weather change did not improve the spirits of a certain gentleman from New Scotland Yard, however. It was a very disgruntled and frustrated Inspector Lestrade who climbed the seventeen steps to our chambers at 221 B. Baker Street. His face was so disconsolate that, after ushering him to the visitor's chair, I hurried to the sideboard and busied myself with decanter and gasogene. Alas, the resultant alcoholic medication to take off the chill had no effect on Lestrade's mood.

"I tell you, Mr. Holmes, 't'is the most discouraging moment of my career. The gambler, Harry Blower, a low rascal if ever there was one, and I've got him right in my hands. Dead to rights as they say, and then he's whisked away from me because of the addled mind of an obstinate woman."

"Best we start from the beginning," said Holmes.

Lestrade took another swallow of his libation and, after a moment of indecision, accepted the Trichinopoli cigar I offered him. As the ferret-faced policeman lit up, it was obvious that he was trying to preserve his composure.

"Harry Blower might not be known to you gentlemen, but he's a rough piece of goods what operates in Lambeth."

The name meant nothing to me. Holmes did not indicate whether it did or not.

"We've been watching this boy for some time fer there's a couple of horse players which come to mysterious ends and the word was that they had been big winners against Blower's book. Then there's some others what is supposed to have tried to run out on a bet with Blower what got bunged up for fair, one of them a fatality."

"He sounds like a sinister citizen indeed," I stated.

"He's that fer sure and he's got some lads from the old Brighton Duster gang for strong arm work plus Gannet the Gimp who is with him night and day to do his talkin'."

I was prompted to question the last remark but remained silent as Lestrade continued his tale of woe.

"To round out the story, we have Frankie Finn who owns a gin shop in Chelsea and is a high roller in betting circles. It is common gossip that Blower is carrying a lot of slips on Finn who evidently had a run of rum luck. Blower, according to the whispers, told Finn to get up the money or else. The 'or else' not being easy for Finn had some tough friends of his own and a little wagering went on as to who was goin' to get who."

Holmes chuckled. "This has all the elements of a tale of the American underworld."

"Well," continued Lestrade as though the admission came hard, "a bookmaker is pretty much forced to collect or he's not in business. But I'll get to the point, Mr. Holmes. Last night Harry Blower paid Finn a visit at his rooming house in Chelsea. My guess is it was a surprise visit or Finn would have had some of his boys with him. Finn's landlady let Blower in and the two of them is in Finn's room when there's an explosion what sounds like a shot to the landlady and she was right. Cool as a cucumber, Blower comes down the stairs and leaves the premises. The landlady, an old crone named Pniddy Dorcus, runs up to Finn's room and finds her boarder dead as they come with a bullet in his head."

"Good heavens, Lestrade," I exclaimed, "if I've ever heard of an open and shut case this is it. What can your problem be?"

"My problem, Doctor, is that I was of your way of thinkin'. I figured Harry Blower had let rage get the best o' him and he'd made that slip we've been waiting fer at the Yard."

"Evidentally this was not the case," said Sherlock Holmes.

"'T'was not, sir, fer Blower, when he left the boarding house, says a real calm and nice 'goodnight.' At least that's what Pniddy Dorcas says happened."

"That is understandable," I argued. "A rascal of Blower's type with more than a passing acquaintance with violence and death could well be calm under the circumstances or pretend to be."

"I'll give you that, Doctor," replied Lestrade. "But how, pray tell, did Blower say goodnight to Pniddy Corcas? His bein' a dummy you see."

Holmes' head was nodding. "I suspected that when you said that he had a henchman, Gannet, to do his talking."

My eyes were shifting from Lestrade to the sleuth and back in a dazed manner.

"Do you mean that this bookmaker is a mute?"
Lestrade nodded. "According to some very reputable members of your profession, sir. Doctor Pierpont Evans for one."

My indecision vanished. "Evans' reputation is beyond question. If he has stated that this Blower fellow is a mute, you can depend upon it."

Lestrade was regarding the master sleuth in a hopeful manner.

"What do you make of it, Mr. 'Olmes?"

The great detective's eyes had shifted to the dancing flames in the hearthfire and when he responded it was almost as though he were talking to himself.

"According to Watson, Blower is incapable of speech so we can accept that as our starting point. Which brings us to the landlady, Priddy Dorcas. Did she imagine that Blower spoke to her? Are his words the product of an aged mind upset by the sound of a shot in her establishment? Could Blower have bought off Priddy to state that he spoke? If so, the bookmaker evolved the most bizarre alibi I've ever heard of."

"But what am I to do, Mr. 'Olmes? The Dorcas woman, simply by testifying that Blower was closeted with Finn and departed after the shot, can hang him. But if she states that he bid her goodnight, the whole case against the gambler goes up in smoke."

"It is certainly a tasty dish you have placed before us, Lestrade," said Holmes with relish. "I'm quite indebted to you. A visit to Priddy Dorcas seems called for and, since she may refuse to speak to me or Watson, best you come with us. Will nine o'clock tomorrow morning suit you?"

Anything would have suited the desperate Lestrade and the sooner the better. So it was that the following morning found the three of us on the steps of a brick house in a reasonably sedate section of Chelsea as yet unaware that murder had been an unwelcome visitor less than forty-eight hours before.

When the substantial oaken door of the rooming house was opened in response to Lestrade's knock, a wrinkled face that radiated suspicion surveyed us. Priddy Dorcas' rawboned features resembled a map of a rocky terrain but she was not lacking in energy and immediately proved it. At the sight of the Inspector, a raspy voice assailed our ears.

"Ah, it be you agin. Well I'm not changin' me tune one note, Mr. Peeler, and you can get me into all the courts in the land and I'll swear on every bible there be as to what happened. You think I be daft but I kncw wot 'appened and I'll tell wot I seen and wot I 'eard just like I tol you ten and five times, you 'ear me? So get ye off!"

As she began to close the door, Lestrade's boot was in the way. With a helpless look he rapidly stammered an introduction.

"Mrs. Dorcas, this here is Sherlock Holmes."

Had he stated that the Queen was in our presence, he

could not have gotten a greater reaction. Priddy Dorcas' gimlet eyes widened and the grim lines of her face were erased by awe.

"'Olmes, the detective," she breathed. "Then this 'ere be Doctor Watson." Rubbing her hands against a soiled skirt she tried to rally a smile and half-way succeeded. Her attempt had a distant kinship with the shyness of a small girl.

Stepping aside, she hesitantly gestured towards the dingy interior of her front hall.

"Would yuh be pleased to step in, gentlemen. I'll be gettin' you a spot of tea right away."

"Well," I thought, "here we go again."

The cold and austere Holmes was habitually distrustful of the opposite sex, especially since the Irene Adler affair. (See: *"A Scandal in Bohemia."*) Yet his courtly manner and piercing eyes consistently had a semi-hypnotic effect on them as though they were in the presence of some greater being partially beyond conception.

"Let us not trouble you to that extent, Mrs. Dorcas," said Holmes as he entered the questionable establishment as though it were the grand ballroom at auckingham. "If you would allow Doctor Watson and myself, along with our mutual friend Inspector Lestrade, a moment of your time, that will suffice."

The woman insisted on taking both Holmes' and my bowlers as she let Lestrade fend for himself.

"This is an honor, sir, fer a fact. Let me be tellin' you, Doctor Watson, many's the time I've walked me way to the Marylebone Library to get me one of yer books 'bout Mr. 'Olmes adventures. Strike me down if 't'is not so."

I mumbled modest words as befits an admired author while we were ushered to three rickety chairs in a semi-dark and tiny sitting room. Outside a frosty wind was blowing from the north and the faded interior, reeking of better days long removed, had a chill to it. I was glad I had not removed my topcoat.

Almost with regret, as though not wishing her meager possessions to be fully revealed, Priddy Dorcas went to the front windows and opened the drapes which had the heartening effect of dispelling the gloom. Then she sat herself on a three-legged stool, regarding Holmes as though waiting for him to say: "Once upon a time." She ignored Lestrade completely.

"Mrs. Dorcas," began Holmes, "the Inspector, here, is in search of the truth which is so oft the only defense of godfearing and law abiding folk against the forces of evil." The sleuth's voice rolled forth in rich, round tones and his rapt audience of one looked as though she had just discovered Santa Claus. "He has told us of your experience so ours is but a visit of confirmation. There is, of course, the possibility that you might recall something else," he added suggestively.

Priddy's jaw firmed as her head shook in a negative fashion but before she could rekindle her dander, Holmes continued.

"I can well understand your consternation. Indeed, your experience could have shattered a less self reliant lady."

Priddy had never considered herself a lady and only half understood the meaning of consternation, but she sensed that Holmes' words referred to a good thing and alien warmth crept back into her eyes.

"Here was Blower, the bookmaker, whom you know by sight and are capable of identifying beyond doubt."

Expecting questions and receiving statements, Priddy could only nod with gratitude. No one had ever considered her as an impeccable source of information before.

"You were shocked by the explosion, as any honest person would be, and then Harry Blower came down the stairs. You saw him clearly and know that it was the same man you admitted to your home."

A nod of affirmation was Holmes' answer.

"Then this known mute..."

"Known what, sir?" asked Priddy.

"Dummy," interjected Lestrade who then regretted his prompting.

But the newfound "lady" paid him no heed.

"He did speak, Mr. 'Olmes. Called me by name, he did. ' Goodnight, Mrs. Dorcas,' he says, smooth as silk. I bloomin' near fell over in a heap and he gives me a wave, lets himself out and 'es gone."

"A shock indeed," said Holmes with an undercurrent of commiseration that I would have given my socks to be able to use with ailing patients.

"It shook me, Mr. 'Olmes, deed it did."

"But you recounted the matter as it happened, which was the right thir'g to do." The sleuth rose carefully from the chair he had been using.".

"We'll be off now, Mrs. Dorcas, with our deep appreciation."

Lestrade and I, who had been listening to Holmes in a dumbfounded manner, had little choice but to follow in the sleuth's footsteps as he made his way to the outer portal. There was a look in Priddy Dorcas' eyes as though she were supressing a flood of questions. All traces of the harridan were gone as she attempted to see us to the door in the manner of a vestal virgin of ancient vintage.

At the curb, as we hailed a carriage, Lestrade regarded Holmes in a puzzled manner.

"Mr. 'Olmes," said the Inspector, "I thought you were going to break down the hag's story."

"She told the truth," replied the sleuth. "I know of Harry Blower and the late Frankie Finn as well. Theirs was almost a territorial dispute and we are in the Finn sphere here. Priddy Dorcas has lack of motive to back up her words. Her interests were best served by being a member of the Finn contingent, as she was. She had no reason to give Harry Blower an alibi, as strange as it might be, which brings us to the solution of this farrago."

"You've solved the case, Mr. 'Olmes?" asked an excited Lestrade.

"Let us say I've had the solution forced upon me," was the sleuth's cryptic response. "Drop in on us 'round fivish and I'll have the matter tidied up for you, Lestrade."

That was all the world's only consulting detective would

reveal. I did not press him for an explanation, well knowing how my intimate friend delighted in his denouements.

Winter darkness was staining the sky when Lestrade again entered our sitting room at 221 B. Baker Street. Sherlock Holmes disentangled the intricacies of the puzzle with an unusually brief preamble.

"Alas, poor Watson here has heard me say it many-a-time. When all else proves impossible, what seems impossible must be true. There is no impossibility relative to this matter but the solution is certainly outrØ. As I indicated previously, there is quite a section of my files devoted to Harry Blower. He was born in Stepney, by the way, a section which I visited this afternoon. After our Chelsea excursion this morning, I was convinced that Priddy Dorcas was telling the truth. She admitted Blower because the meeting was probably arranged. Finn felt no peril being on his home grounds. No one came with Blower. Only one possibility remained that could explain the Dorcus woman's story. Blower has a twin brother who is not a mute and such fact was born out by the Stepney Hall of Records and a fortunate interview with a local midwife. Two men will go on trial for the murder of Finn, Lestrade. Find the brother that Blower has kept secret in case of need and your mystery is solved."

The solution of the murder of Frankie Finn proved one of the highlights of Inspector Lestrade's career though, as in "The Case of the Six Napoleons," Lestrade lauded Holmes' brillance to the skies and spoke of it often at Scotland Yard. He did not, however, choose to mention it to the journalists.

THE COUNTERFEIT CAROT

Sherlock Holmes had just concluded his second major case of the year when Spring arrived, belatedly, and he was for the moment at liberty.

It was mid-evening at 221B Baker Street. Mrs. Hudson had cleared away the dishes and I was settled at the escritoire, savoring a Trichinopoly cigar, and attempting to sort out notes on the most recent case which I hoped to make available to my readers.

Holmes had been seated before the hearth fire gazing at the dancing flames but he soon wearied of this and rose to restlessly pace 'round our sitting room before positioning himself by the bow window to stare at the night scene. Finally a deep sigh escaped him as he turned from his vantage point.

"What can be troubling you? Holmes," I inquired. Actually, my words reeked of hypocrisy. I well knew that my friend's hair trigger brain was yearning for the challenge of a puzzle, the excitement of the chase. It made little sense since his career was certainly approaching its zenith at this point and his name was not only legend in his native land. His reputation as the greatest deductive mind of his time was world-wide but Holmes was not one to dwell on past triumphs and constantly yearned for fresh problems in which to insert the scapel of his specialized knowledge. My face rose from my work in a resigned manner, expecting to find my friend testy and chafing at the bit. He surprised me, not for the first time I might add. There was a wry smile on his hawk-like face and a shrug of acceptance stirred his shoulders as he strolled towards the bookcase.

"I must, not willingly, bow to the inevitable, Watson. The aura is not right. The night, though chilly, is clear as crystal. No approaching storm nor the possibility of fog. So I assume that fate intends for us to spend a peaceful evening in our snug bachelor quarters with no call to sally forth on the trail of wrongdoers."

With this unusual statement, Holmes extracted his Common-Place book from a shelf and flung himself on the couch, fumbling in his dressing gown pocket for his short briar. Bless me if he did not seem prepared to accept inactivity in a philosophical manner rather than rant about the dearth of imaginative crime since the fall of the late Professor Moriarty.

For once, his prediction proved wrong, possibly because my friend's star of destiny saw fit to reward him for a rare exhibition of patience.

There was a knock on the door and then the figure of Billy, our page boy, was revealed on the landing outside.

"A Mr. Courtland Gould, sir, in 'opes yuh might spare 'im a few moments."

"Indeed I shall. Show him up by all means."

The smile of delight, which had creased Holmes face at the prospect of a visitor, soured somewhat when he turned towards me.

"I trust I can deal with the gentleman's problem in better fashion than my attempt to foretell our activities of this evening."

"You feel that he is a client, then?"

"Hardly the hour for soliciting church funds," replied the sleuth dryly as he crossed to the mantel to stock his pipe with shag from the Persian slipper.

Our visitor was youngish, his face very fair, with a slight, reddish moustache. There were the remains of freckles upon his cheeks and his grey eyes were sunken. The lines around his mouth might have been etched by pain, a supposition reinforced by the way he leaned on his stick and favored his right leg. With my medical instincts aroused, I made haste to indicate the comfortable cane-back by the fire and offer a libation which he accepted in a tentative manner.

"Awfully good of you to see me, Mr. Holmes."

"I pride myself at being available to those in need," replied the sleuth somewhat formally. "Though I fancy the idea of coming here was a spur-of-the-moment decision."

"How did you ever arrive at that conclusion?" asked Gould.

"You have just completed a train trip for there is a smudge of dust on your hat that is indigenous to the British railway system. Also, I note the stub of a ticket winking at me from your waistcoat pocket of the 'and return' variety. Therefore, London was your point of origin so you did not journey here to see me. Assuming your headquarters are in the metropolis, had you anticipated enlisting my services, you would have made some prior attempt via cable or message to ascertain that I was on the premises."

As Gould accepted a whiskey and water, I noted the affirmation in his eyes. It was that familiar look indicating that it was all so obvious once my friend had outlined the logical path which his meticulous mind had followed.

"I am a Commission Agent, Mr. Holmes, and journeyed to Sussex today relative to a matter brought to my attention. Since things took a strange twist, I decided to come here from the station for I am sorely puzzled."

Holmes, through a cloud of smoke, regarded Gould approvingly. The man seemed disposed to get to the matter without hemming and hawing. The world's only consulting detective tended to be brusque if forced to coax essentials from unwilling throats.

"But yesterday, Mr. Holmes, I was approached by one Simon Keene, an American gentleman engaged in rather the same line of work that I am. He wished me to negotiate with Lord

Tyrell for the purchase of Carot's painting, 'Belle Dame.'"

"Since Lord Tyrell resides at his country estate in Sussex, I take it that you undertook the commission. With no suspicion, of course."

"Suspicion of what?" I asked without intending to.

"That particular Carot painting is hanging in the Louvre in Paris at this moment," replied Holmes, indicating no annoyance at my interruption.

"I was unaware of that fact, Mr. Holmes," replied Gould, "but Lord Tyrell quickly informed me that his painting was but a copy of the work of the French master."

"And his Lordship was quite surprised at the amount you offered for the copy," said Holmes.

Gould choked on his drink. "That's exactly what happened."

Since I was also registering surprise, Holmes explained, directing his words to our visitor.

"You are here, sir, with a problem. It could only be puzzlement over the amount offered for a bogus masterpiece. I assume you are also wondering if your client, Keene, is aware that Lord Tyrell's painting is not the real Corot."

"That question did cross my mind," admitted Gould. "But then, it would seem illogical that Keene, representing a tycoon like Huntington, would not know the facts about the art work he was commissioned to secure."

"So your client is acting on behalf of the American rail magnate. I agree with your analysis unless Keene is a fool indeed."

"He did not strike me as being that, Mr. Holmes."

"What was the amount involved?"

"One thousand pounds."

For some reason, Gould's answer pleased Holmes. His next words clued me as to why.

"This does present points of interest. First, you are instructed to approach Lord Tyrell to buy his painting, 'Belle Dame' by Corot but the offering price would not come close to securing the genuine painting. Yet, for a copy, it is a generous sum. Then we have the problem of why Mr. Keene did not undertake to contact Lord Tyrell himself."

"He did explain that, in a fashion. Said that in matters of art, the Americans have a reputation for being gullible. In addition, he thought the matter might be effected more promptly if his Lordship was contacted by a fellow countryman. I rather sensed that Keene is awed by titles and possibly at sea as to how to behave in the presence of one."

"Quite possible," admitted Holmes. "Another question. Lord Tyrell is reputed to have a considerable collection of objects d'art. Why would he be in possession of a copy? Is it signed, by the way?"

"Yes, sir, though not by its creator. The name of Corot is affixed to the oil."

"An out and out counterfeit then," said Holmes.

"Lord Tyrell came across it in France. He referred to it as a tourist trap but was taken by the ability of the unknown forger. He picked it up as a curio."

Holmes rose to his feet suddenly, crossing to the mantle to lean against it in a familiar position.

"The thought has to arise that his Lordship's painting might be the genuine article." Before Gould could make a comment, the sleuth continued.

"Extremely unlikely, however, so let us dismiss that idea for the nonce. Keene gave no indication that Lord Tyrell's painting was not genuine?"

"None, sir. I assumed that he was making an offer for a painting that he hoped to secure for one thousand pounds. Lord Tyrell cleared up the matter for me."

"Complicating your commission at the same time. What was his Lordship's reaction to Keene's proposal?"

"He is agreeable with the understanding that the purchaser accepts the painting as a counterfeit."

Again Gould's response satisfied Holmes. "The American, doubtless, has made arrangements about contacting you?"

"Tomorrow morning, Mr. Holmes."

"Tell him what you have just related to me. That his Lordship is prepared to sell with the proviso that the painting is accepted as a counterfeit."

Gould seemed disappointed. "That's all there is to it?"

"Not quite. I would be interested in Keene's reaction as well as his further instructions."

So the matter stood. Gould made his way to his waiting hansom and Holmes knocked the dottle from his briar and switched to his cherrywood. Since he gave no indication of plunging into deep thought, I pursued the matter for I shared Gould's puzzlement.

"What do you make of this matter, Holmes?"

"Deep waters, old fellow. Especially since Simon Keene knows the painting is not genuine."

"You seem awfully sure of that."

"The introduction of the American millionaire, Huntington, clues me there. The rail tycoon is buying Gainsborough, Romney, Reynolds and paying top prices. He would not have, as a representative, some dolt ignorant of the fact that the 'Belle Dame' is in the Louvre."

"Agreed. If Keene actually is in the employ of Mr. Huntington."

Holmes surveyed me with an approving smile. "Our years together have developed a suspicious nature in you, old friend. Your remark is very much to the point."

"If Keene is not acting on behalf of the American collector, why does he want this counterfeit?"

"Why indeed?"

"You know, it does seem like the Tyrell painting might be the real thing. What a coup if it could be acquired for a mere thousand pounds."

"I will check that out with a cable to a contact in Paris. An unproductive investigation I fear, but necessary none the less. More to the point will be the action Keen decides on tomorrow."

That being all I could get out of my friend, I retired for

the night, anxious to learn what the new day would reveal regarding this puzzling matter.

It was shortly after breakfast when Mr. Gould returned to our quarters. His manner was apologetic as he revealed his news.

"Mr. Holmes, I should never have approached you regarding this matter at all. It was but a wild thought and you have my apologies."

"Come, come," said my friend in the soothing voice he used so well. "I've found this adventure of yours quite provocative."

"But of no import since, like one of your amazing deductions, it all fits together once explained."

"You've seen Simon Keene, of course."

Gould indicated that this was so. "I followed your instructions and Keene wasn't surprised at all. In fact, his reply rather put me down. He stated that Lord Tyrell's painting was certainly a copy, the original being so well known that everyone was aware that it was a possession of the French government. His being right didn't help my attitude so I asked him point blank what interest an American millionaire had in a known counterfeit."

Gould paused and Holmes, his eyes alight with interest, prompted him.

"And his explaination?"

"He was really quite sporty about it, agreeing that I had reason to be puzzled. He then informed me that Mr. Huntington was planning on a room of his collection devoted to forgeries and that was the reason for his interest in the bogus Corot."
The agent regarded Holmes anxiously. "He wasn't pulling my leg, was he, sir?"

"Not at all. Huntington has acquired several spurious manuscripts supposedly by Dickens and an excellent forgery of a Mark Twain letter. Also, an imitation Gutenberg Bible I understand."

"Keene explained the matter so readily I assumed it was

the truth." Gould sighed. "That's it, then."

"Not quite," replied Holmes. "What is your next move?"

"To consummate the deal with Lord Tyrell. The American gave me one thousand pounds for which I gave him a receipt, of course. He also penned a statement that, in purchasing the painting, he was conscious of the fact that it was a copy."

"Very business-like. Did Keene pay your fee, by the way?"

"Fifty pounds. Another fifty on receipt of the painting in my office."

"Ten percent which is standard." Holmes made note of Gould's place of business. "Now, sir, proceed with the arrangements with Lord Tyrell. Best go to Sussex and bring the painting yourself."

"Mr. Keene specified that. He wishes the frame as well."

"Does he now? That's interesting. You go ahead with the matter and arrange for Keene to meet you at your office when you return with the painting and frame."

Holmes' manner indicated that the meeting was over and Gould rose slowly, looking at my friend with a native shrewdness which had become increasingly evident the more I saw of him.

"There's more to it than that, isn't there, Mr. Holmes?"

"Oh, yes. You'll receive a visit from an Inspector Lestrade. He'll explain the situation to you and take charge of the matter."

Gould seemed reluctant to leave. "Regarding your efforts in this matter..." he began.

Holmes waved this aside with an airy gesture. "We'll not go into that. I found the whole affair of benefit as mental stimulation. Good day to you, sir."

As Gould made his way slowly down the seventeen steps leading to our first floor quarters, I viewed Holmes with an exaspiration fostered by the instincts of my Scotch forebears.

"You are frightfully prompt about refusing fees, you know."

"Hardly cricket in this case, Watson."

I was about to inquire as to the meaning of this statement when Holmes chose to be revealing.

"Last night and early this morning I busied myself and my diligence bore fruit." He slid open the desk drawer, extracting several cablegrams. "Here is information from a contact of mine in Pasadena, California."

Holmes read the message to me. "Huntington Museum has no interest in spurious paintings. Keene unknown at this end."

As my friend's eyes rose to mine I sputtered excitedly. "I thought so. This chap, Keene, is up to no good."

Holmes indicated another cable. "From Paris I am assured that the genuine Corot is in the Louvre."

"Ah hah!"

"Now see what you make of this, old friend. Three years ago, the Tyrell sapphires were stolen. Though it was suspected that one of the servants was the culprit, the famous necklace was never found. I collected quite a file on the matter wondering if the sapphires would ever resurface."

"Why, Holmes, it is as plain as the nose on your face."

"That's pretty plain, Watson. What deductions do you arrive at?"

I stumbled over myself in my eagerness. "It's Keene, of course. He was the thief. The reason why he wants to buy a worthless painting is the frame, for I noted that you made a point of that when it was mentioned."

"Right on, Watson. You are doing fine."

"The reason the necklace was never found is because it never left the Tyrell mansion. Keene secreted it in the frame of the picture. Now he wants to recover his loot. You've arranged for this naive Gould chap to bring the picture and frame to his office where Keene will take possession but Lestrade will be secreted on the premises and catch the thief red handed."

"Watson, you never cease to amaze me. However, the suspect servant in the Tyrell mansion was one Loring Grant. He was convicted of another robbery and sentenced to a lengthy term in Princetown which he never completed, for he died better than a year ago."

I buried my face in my hands with a groan. "But now my

theory of the thief bent on recovering his loot vanishes into thin air."

"Not completely. Someone else might have learned of Grant's secreting the necklace in the picture frame. Fortunately, there was a definite clue."

"I fail to see it."

"Think, Watson! Something about the matter is amiss." Drat it, Holmes let me puzzle over the matter till the following day. Even then I was informed of the denouement by the press. Holmes was absent on some matter and I confronted him with the afternoon papers upon his return.

"What does this mean?" I demanded of him, waving the front page angrily. "Tyrell sapphires recovered. Inspector Alec MacDonald of New Scotland Yard secures famed necklace and apprehends Tricky Ted Trampas, well known confidence man, on Surrey express." I found myself breathing deeply. "Who is Tricky Ted and where was Lestrade?"

"Let us remain calm, old fellow," responded my friend hastily. There was concern in his eyes intermingled with a twinkle promoted by my indignant attitude. "Your reconstruction of the case was fine as far as it went. Did I not say, just the other day, that what seems at first glance so obvious frequently does not stand up under detailed analysis? Your thoughts paralleled mine up to that point. Then I received a cablegram which I can quote: 'Assume one Courtland Gould has contacted you at my suggestion. Do you have any thoughts regarding matter? Signed Tyrell.'"

I sank onto the couch in astonishment. "What does that mean?"

"Simply that Gould's visit here was prompted by Lord Tyrell, a fact which he did not mention. Some years past, I was of assistance to his Lordship's now deceased wife and when this matter came up, Lord Tyrell thought of me."

"That makes sense. Anticipating that his Lordship might contact you, Gould came here immediately upon his return from Sussex."

"Now you are beginning to glimpse the true picture. You

need but one clue to bring you into focus. The Tyrell sapphires were stolen over three years ago. The thief, Loring Grant, died in prison. If someone knew his secret, the hiding place of the necklace, why did they not attempt to secure it sooner? Answer, because they could not do so, which led me to investigate the identity of Grant's ceilmate at Princetown."

"Tricky Ted Trampas," I muttered.

"Correct, and he was released a month ago. No injured leg, but otherwise he fits the description of our client, Courtland Gould. Gould established a false identity, for he is a cautious chap and a bunko artist as well. Then he approached Lord Tyrell. If something went amiss with his Lordship, it was the non-existent client, Keene, that the police would look for.

"Tyrell, somewhat suspicious of the affair, brought my name into the matter and Gould altered his plans. He decided to use me as a means of calming his Lordship's misgivings and was delighted when I took his bait, arranging to have Lestrade at his office to apprehend Keene. Keene never existed, of course. Gould secured the painting and the precious frame containing the sapphires with the intention of taking the necklace from its hiding place and vanishing. I had MacDonald on his trail and the dependable Scot was able to nab him at that moment when he removed the sapphires from the frame."

I was disconsolate, chiding myself for being obtuse, but managed to rally bravely. "It is a shame, Holmes, that you did not accept a fee from Tricky Ted. That would have been a bitter pill for the rascal to swallow."

"Let us not be greedy, Watson. The reward that Lord Tyrell has offered for the return of his famous necklace should be enough to satisfy even your frugal nature."

THE ELMSWORTH TIARA

A fierce wind, spawned in the tractless artic wastelands of the north, had buffeted London all day. However, as the winter sun sank in the west, the gale subsided to be replaced by a dead calm that should have been a warning.

Down Baker Street and elsewhere in the great metropolis of six millions, tendrils of fog crept, advance guard for the vast blanket of swirling yellowish-white that soon enveloped the city and environs. The houses opposite 221B faded from view, obscured by a moist, cloying eiderdown and it was as though we were alone in the world, our residence shipwrecked in a sea of misty nothingness.

Holmes was leafing his way through his case book of that year as I stirred up the hearthfire with a poker, for a damp and penetrating cold had infiltrated the stout walls of our bachelor abode. We were quite unprepared for the appearance of Mrs. Hudson at our door with news of visitors, since not only sight but the sound of infrequent traffic without had been cut off by the atmospheric intruder.

Our patient landlady was indicating in the direction of the seventeen steps leading to our first floor threshold in an excited manner and she spoke in hushed tones.

"I'm quite beside myself, Mr.'Olmes fer 'tis Lord and Lady Elmsworth what's below requesting some moments of yer time.

That Lestrade person be with 'em."

Mrs. Hudson's last sentence was delivered with a disapproving sniff. She had resented the ferret-like Scotland Yard Inspector since the Jefferson Hope matter which Holmes had solved but Lestrade got the credit for. Happily, my recounting of the matter in print under the title of "A Study In Scarlet" had given the true facts to the public.

"Do show them up, Mrs. Hudson," said Holmes with a smile."We must not keep the nobility cooling their heels."

Shortly thereafter Lond Elmsworth and his smashingly attractive wife occupied our best chairs with Lestrade hovering in the background as though in fear that there might be a breach of etiquette.

"Jolly decent of you seeing us with no notice at all," mumbled his Lordship. Though I gave the society columns short shrift, I could not be ignorant of our titled visitors since it was a rare London social event that they did not attend.

"My door is always open for those with problems," stated Holmes almost automatically. It was a phrase he had used many times. Eager to get to the matter at hand, the sleuth cut through possible preambles.

"I assume the tiara has been stolen. When and where pray tell?"

His Lordship's jaw dropped and Lady Elmsworth gave vent to a short, nervous laugh.

"Surely you could not have heard of the occurence. But aother example of your famous deductive reasoning though, if you want my opinion, you are blessed with an intuition, supposedly the province of my sex," she said. I noticed that her Ladyship had a determined jaw and recalled that she was American, the daughter of a Colorado silver king.

"Lady Elmsworth, surely you jest. You and his Lordship contact Sherlock Holmes in the compan.y of an Inspector from new Scotland Yard. Not about the Charity Ball next week I'll wager which leaves us with the famous Elmsworth Tiara. When did it happen?"

"Last night, " replied his Lordship. " I was rather insistent with the Commissioner that the matter not become public knowledge. Inspector Lestrade has been assigned to the case, off the record, as 'twere. My good wife is an avid follower of your career, Mr. Holmes, and she can be insistent as well."

I noted Holmes and Lestrade exchange a quick glance, the meaning of which eluded me. Then Holmes prompted Lord Elmsworth to give him the details but it was Her Ladyship who seized the conversational ball.

"We dined at home last night,Mr.Holmes, with a guest, Dr. Max Bauer."

Now it was I who exchanged a meaningful look with the great sleuth. We knew Dr. Bauer well since the gem expert had been helpful in the matter of "The Golden Bird."

"The tiara was in the house, and considering Bauer's reputation..."

When Her Ladyship terminated her explanation, half said, I realized how alert she was for she had read Holmes' expression, not an easy thing to do.

"But then, you would be familiar with the gentleman, Mr. Holmes."

"Indeed. Dr. Bauer is an old friend. His book on famous gems is a classic. It would be strange indeed if he did not wish to see the tiara."

"I secured it from my bedroom," continued her Ladyship. "Dr.Bauer, upon inspecting it, told us as diplomatically as he could that it was a copy and that the gems were ersatz."

His Lordship now contributed to the revelation. "We had taken the tiara from the vault in the City and Suburban that very day. Naturally we all rushed up to my wife's bedroom. It was then that Grace noted a lamp on her desk that was not in its usual position. We discovered that the window behind it was unlocked and immediately became suspicious. When any of the Elmsworth collection is on the premises, we take suitable precautions."

"You feel, then, that the real tiara was stolen last evening and a copy left in its place? Possibly while you were dining with

Dr. Bauer?"

"That was our thought," admitted His Lordship. "I put through a call to the Commissioner of Police and shortly thereafter Inspector Lestrade was on the scene."

All eyes swiveled towards the Inspector who took up the narrative.

"The bedroom is on the first floor but there is ivy on the exterior wall that grows close to the window in question. If it was locked, and His Lordship assured me that it was as did the butler, I don't know how the thief unlocked it. There was no broken glass or any sign of tampering with the frame. I did find a footprint at the base of the ivy made by a size twelve workshoe."

I had the feeling that Lestrade had more to tell but he lapsed into silence and the Elmsworths turned to Holmes as though expecting him to produce a solution with no further ado.

The sleuth rose from the Queen Anne chair by the fire, a not too subtle indication that the meeting was over.

"Watson and I will view the premises tomorrow for there is little we can do tonight. I'm sure the Inspector has uncovered all the available clues but possibly he might go over the scene with us?"

"Of course," mumbled Lestrade.

After our visitors descended to their waiting carriage, I tried to sound Holmes out as to his thoughts regarding the matter.

"Why would His Lordship use his not inconsiderable influence to keep this robbery under wraps, Holmes?"

"Nothing unreasonable there. He and his wife are involved in a number of charities and at events in connection with them. Lady Elmsworth generally wears some of the family jewels. This was not the usual robbery, Watson, in that a counterfeit tiara was part of the plot. If word of this leaks out, can you not imagine curious ladies of fashion wondering if they are viewing the Elmsworth gems or replicas of them? A public display of famous jewels is a drawing card, old friend, but a breath of suspicion dulls the appeal."

Holmes was indisposed to discuss the case further.

Early the following morning I found myself, with my intimate friend and Lestrade, surveying the exterior of the Elmsworth Mansion on Collingsgate Square. Lestrade had pointed out the window through which it was assumed the thief had made his entry. The ivy growing close to it was not profuse.

"Now I see what's on your mind," said Holmes to the Inspector."That ivy wouldn't support a midget."

"If we are to believe this footprint, we're not dealing with a small person," stated the policeman as he led us closer to bed from which the ivy grew and covered it with burlap as well. Drawing this aside, he revealed the large imprint of a shoe, clearly defined in the soft, loamy soil.

Holmes was crouched close to the imprint in a trice and from the pocket of his inverness he extracted a tape measure which he put to use.

"I knew this clue would make Mr. 'O.lmes 'appy," whispered Lestrade. "He do seem to have a passion for footprints and such."

I had to nod in agreement, my mind going to the Study In Scarlet case and the matter of the Rangoon Jade.

After several minutes, Holmes rose to his feet and rejoined us with a satisfied air.

"Would you be wantin'to see Her Ladyship's bedroom, Mr.Holmes?" asked Lestrade.

"Not right now," replied the sleuth.

"Well, if you're finished here, what's your next move?"

"Assuming that Dr.Bauer is still in England, I think some words with him would not be amiss."

Since this told Lestrade nothing, his face registered disappointment and Holmes took pity on him.

"I should mention," he said, "that the footprint was made by a MacKlintock work shoe. They feature a distinctive sole pattern, you see."

"Where does that get us?" asked Lestrade.

"It is a heavily built type of footwear, not practical for

anyone of small stature or weight."

"That seems reasonable, it being a work boot," I said, wishing to be a part of the discussion.

"And yet," replied Holmes surveying both Lestrade and myself with twinkling eyes,"that indentation is so shallow that it had to be made by someone of no more that seven and a half stone."

Having completely mystified both the Inspector and myself, Holmes hailed a hansom crossing Collingsgate Square and I plodded patiently in his wake. It was obvious, to me at least, that my friend had some definite ideas about the fate of the Elmsworth Tiara.

Busy with patient calls in the late morning, I returned to 221B Baker Street to find the rolypoly figure of Dr. Max Bauer in our sitting room closeted with Holmes. Bauer's book, "Precious Stones" published in 1896 is considered one of the most comprehensive studies of gems ever written. The doctor's hair was as unruly as I remembered it.

"Ach, Vatson. Now we get down to business. Maybe your detective friend lets me know vat it iss he vants to know."

"Don't let Bauer josh you, Watson, for he has been here but a moment. What I want to know about is the Elmsworth Tiara."

"Hmmmmm, undt I dined mit der Elmsworths two nights ago. Veil, never mind dot. Der iss a story vat goes mit der tiara. During der French Revolution, three of der crown jewels of France vas stolen. Two of them, the Regent undt der Sancy, surfaced later. So did the third stone, a rare blue diamond, but it had been cut. Der larger part showed up after some years but not der smaller. Der iss a theory dat der main gem in der Elmsworth Tiara is der missing piece."

"Good heavens,"I exclaimed,"that would make the tiara valuable indeed."

"I vould appraise it at twenty-five thousand pounds," replied Bauer. He was very casual about this more than considerable sum. "Dat vas der value Streeter placed on it undt I concur vit him."

"How does Edwin Streeter, the royal jeweler, figure in this?" I asked.

"He vas hired by Inter-Ocean Insurance to evaluate the Elmsworth collection yen der policy vas taken out by his Lordship."

"Did Streeter actually see the tiara?" asked Holmes. There was that predatory look about him at this moment that I knew so well.

"Nein. Strange you should ask dat. It vas not available ven der appraisal vas made. Der rest of the Elmsworth jewels iss not zoo yell known as der tiara.Streeter had to actually inspect dem to estimate der value but he could appaise der tiara by its reputation alone, just as I could."

"About your evening with Lord Elmsworth and Her Ladyship," said Holmes. "Is there any chance you might have been fooled by the counterfeit?"

"Kein gednake," said Bauer forcefully.

"Beg pardon," I said, startled.

"Nonsense iss vat I mean, Doctor Vatson. Dat paste vould not fool me for a moment."

"But there is only one Dr. Max Bauer," said Holmes diplomatically. "Would the erzatz tiara fool Watson here or me?"

The German gem expert regarded Holmes for a long moment.

"I see vat you iss driving towards. For a counterfeit, it vas pretty ghood piece of york. Yes...it could fool der non-expert."

Holmes appeared satisfied and while much more was said in a reminiscent vein, that concluded the discussion relative to the Elmsworth Tiara. Bauer promised to contact us on his next visit to England and, with regrets, we finally said farewell to the jovial German who so resembled a character out of Dickens' "Pickwick Papers."

"Well, Watson," said Holmes, rubbing his hands together like a satisfied Shylock, "I have but to contact Inter-Ocean Insurance and we can rid ourselves of this trivial affair."

"Trivial?" I exclaimed? "An object worth twenty-five thousand pounds."

"Considerably more to Lord Elmsworth."

"Do you know where it is?"

"No, but I know what happened to it. But then, I've suspicioned that since the case was first presented to us."

"Come now, Holmes."

"I will accept coincidence but not when it is stretched beyond the breaking point. Lord Elmsworth said that he had taken the tiara from his bank vault the very day of Dr. Bauer's visit. How convenient. That same night a swagman decided to steal the tiara. Rather daring with the mansion occupied and a party in progress."

"He was lucky."

"But unlucky in that Bauer was the guest. That spiked the counterfeit tiara idea."

"Holmes, I can make no sense out of any of this. Who was the burglar?"

"He doesn't exist. Elmsworth went to the City and Suburban Bank, no doubt, but the tiara had already been removed."

Sensing that my confusion was only increasing, Holmes patiently went at the matter from the beginning.

"Both parties to the marriage of the dashing English Lord and the daughter of the American silver king acted on incorrect assumptions. The silver market broke some time back and the fortune of Lady Elmsworth's father went with it. Lord Elmsworth was one of the unfortunate investors in that Netherlands-Sumatra swindle and I'm given to understand that he is singularly unlucky in selecting equines to wager on as well. The mansion on Collingsgate Square is mortgaged to the hilt as is the family estate in Surrey."

"You mean they are both stony?"

"Exactly. The tiara was broken up and sold, stone by stone but the Elmsworths had a copy made to keep up appearances."

"Why did they ever agree to show it to Doctor Bauer?"

"They wanted him to see it, good fellow. He was the one

person sure to brand it as spurious. Thus leading to the supposed robbery and the footprint they had planted to give credence to the idea of the burglar. Having Bauer spot the counterfeit gave the whole scheme an authentic air."

"Of course. And their involving you in the matter was for the same reason."

Holmes nodded. "They felt it would help cast them in the role of the innocents though, in the parlance of the theatre, they overplayed that bit and it was their undoing."

"So it was a plot to collect the insurance money."

"Thus making the tiara pay off in two ways."

I don't know how Holmes arranged it but Inter-Ocean, a frequent client of the sleuth, did not pay the face value of the policy on the Elmesworth Tiara. Lord and Lady Elmsworth did not appear in court on conspiracy charges and the entire matter never reached the newspapers. However, Lord Elmsworth did not offer Sherlock Holmes a fee for his association with the case. That was of no matter since Inter-Ocean was suitably grateful.

THE DIAMOND STUDS

Another holiday season had come and gone. The schedule of the world's greatest detective, Sherlock Holmes, had been unusually clear, a good thing, for we had been quite busy. Holmes was not socially inclined but there were certain meetings which could not be avoided. We had attended a party at the Diogenes Club given by Holmes' brother, Mycroft Holmes, the second most powerful man in England. Present was the Prime Minister and a number of influential government figures. A party at the home of Police Commissioner Brickstone allowed us to exchange season's greetings with Lestrade, Hopkins, Gregson and MacDonald of the Yard. Lord Cantlemere paid us a holiday visit in our chambers at the same time that Jimmie Valentine dropped by with a gift. I wondered what would have happened if the irascible Lord, one of Holmes' greatest admirers, had learned that he brushed elbows with the world's greatest safecracker. That group of former rascals were in evidence, of course. Slim Gilligan, Swifty Summers, Slippery Styles and Get Rich Wallingford all dropped by. One might say that our Christmas was highlighted by a strange cross section of London society.

It took the greater part of a day to tidy up our quarters and it was that very evening that I put aside my copy of an early edition and addressed myself to Sherlock Holmes who was gazing into the flames of the hearth fire.

"I say, Holmes, things have been a bit slack of late in the deduction department, have they not?"

"The inventiveness of the criminal classes seems to have fallen, with Moriarty, into the abyss of the Falls of Reichenback," he replied in a bored tone. "Even the supposedly superior practitioners of fraud, mahem and thievery display a singular lack of judgement. As an instance, the very case that interests you right now."

Despite our many years together, my jaw dropped in amazement. Holmes indulged in a chuckle. "The news story that caught your attention is duplicated in a journal I just read. The matter of the diamond studs, of course."

"How did you know?"

"Aside from the fact that you scrutinized the story intently, taking the trouble to re-read parts of it, there was your tentative overture to test and see if the matter was of interest to me."

"I fear I am obvious," I mumbled.

"Let us say that as a dissembler you are not at your best. In any case, the theft of the studs belonging to Gertrude, Dowager Countess of Parle, does intrigue me."

"They are of great value?"

"Considerable, which makes the robbery newsworthy and a source of annoyance to Scotland Yard since our official friends have made little progress. Singular, since it is obvious that Galantine is the culprit."

Again I registered astonishment, nothing unusual for one associated with the world's greatest detective.

"See here, Holmes, you have but read a newspaper account of the matter and already you can name the culprit?"

"Of course. My mention of a lack of judgement by leading criminals specifically referred to Galantine. He is a Frenchman, born in Normandy, who has enjoyed considerable success. Aside from one incarceration at an early age, he has staged a series of successful jewelry robberies all the while evading the clutches of the Surete Francaise and our people as well."

"Doesn't that indicate talent?" I asked.

"To a point. He has triumphed up to now by using a certain modus operandi so he associates it with success, never realizing that each repetition places a stamp on the job. In stealing the Countess' studs, he might as well have left a business card. Entry by way of a window, the glass cut with a diamond and removed with a suction cup. Rubber surgical gloves, hence no fingerprints. I identified him without difficulty because of his trademark."

"Shouldn't you notify Scotland Yard?"

"They know it is the Frenchman's work but proof is another matter."

Suddenly Holmes' head turned towards our outer door. "Footsteps, Watson, and I recognize the tread. T'is Inspector Tobias Gregson and I'll wager he's here regarding the diamonds of the Countess."

Holmes was right, of course. No sooner had the tall, whitefaced Inspector seated himself than he launched into his lament.

"It's Galentine again, Mr. Holmes."

"The diamond studs matter?"

"Exactly. Devilish thing about it is we almost had him."

"That is an unusual development." The ennui Holmes had displayed vanished.

"Knowing your fancy for strange situations I had to darken your doorway with this one," stated the Inspector, running one hand through his flaxen hair.

"With the added possibility of a solution," murmured Holmes. Then his somewhat brusque manner evaporated. "But let us hear this singular tale."

"The Countess lives on Cannought Street, not the old family residence, for I fear she has experienced financial difficulties in recent years. I had been on a surviellance in the area and was passing her residence last night with two of my men when we noted a cape clad figure leave Lady Gertrude's house. We thought little of it until the figure made note of us and, of a sudden, bolted. We took after him and, rounding a corner, definitely saw the figure duck into the Ponsbey Pub. It is a corner building with entrances on Cannought and Vesely Street as well. In a trice I had one of my men covering the Vesely Street side." The Inspector paused for a moment, seemingly ready to reveal an unusual fact but Holmes beat him to it.

"Serendipity certainly graces your efforts, Gregson, and I can see a pattern emerging. Your associate had the second entrance to the Ponsbey covered before your quarry could pass through the crowded bar and escape. Therefore you had him bottled up, for I know of that pub and there are no other exits."

"Right you are, Mr. Holmes. Only windows face on Cannought and Vesely. The other two walls are solid masonry abutting adjacent buildings."

"It would seem that you had Galentine like a rat in a trap but such was not the case or you would not be here now."

"For a fact," agreed Gregson with a sorrowful expression. "I signalled for additional men and entered the Ponsbey. It has a bit of a shady reputation but everything seemed in order within."

"But no Galantine," said Holmes. "Of course you

searched."

"Every nook and cranny," replied the Inspector.

"All right," said Holmes thoughtfully, "now cast your mind back. You entered the pub. Your man on Vesely Street had orders to allow no one to exit." Gregson was nodding and Holmes continued.

"Your other man stood guard at the Cannought Street door. Now what happened?" There was that opaque look in Holmes' eyes and I knew he was prepared to recreate the moment from the Inspector's words.

"Well, sir, I checked out the patrons, looking for the Frenchman of course, and took a look behind the bar to make sure he wasn't hiding there. I decided to wait until reinforcements arrived before searching the second story."

"But you did inspect the ground floor?"

"Promptly," replied Gregson.

"The men's room?" I asked with a sudden thought. "Empty," said Gregson.

"I say," I continued, "now we come to an embarrassing moment."

Gregson laughed. "T'is the ladies' comfort station you're thinking of, Doctor. A woman came out of it and I was prepared to give it the once over when another lady went in. So I waited till she vacated the area and then investigated. Also empty."

"About the woman in the restroom when you entered?" "We let her go. Perkings got her name," added Gregson, referring to his official notebook. "A Mrs. Gallant."

"What about the second woman?" quiered Holmes.

"Miss Mergatroid. Lives in the neighborhood. Has a knick-knack shop and sells greeting cards and such."

"You interrogated the others present to no avail and so the matter stands."

"That's it, Mr. Holmes. But the figure that we saw had to be Galantine. The robbery occurred at that time. He couldn't just vanish."

"When you have eliminated the impossible, whatever remains, however improbably, must be the truth." Holmes directed a faint smile in my direction. "Watson has heard me say that before."

"You mean the Frenchman simply disappeared?" persisted Gregson.

"In a sense," stated Holmes. There was that removed look in his eyes that indicated he intended to be non-revealing and Gregson recognized it.

"What am I to do, sir?"

"Use the knowledge at your disposal. First a check on the movements of VonSeddar, the Dutch jeweler, is called for. VonSeddar handles Galentine's loot. Also bear in mind that the Frenchman always gets rid of his spoils at the earliest opportunity. Like the assassin who jettisons his weapon immediately."

"Would there be any other thought you have in mind?" asked the Inspector tentatively, as though not really expecting further information from the great consulting detective.

"I shall be in touch on the morrow," said Holmes shortly and I sensed that he was impatient to sort out facts in the recesses of his splendid mind. Gregson, though still at sea, seemed to draw solace from the fact that Holmes was hot on the scent and departed into the night.

The following morning a limpid winter sun did little to alleviate the freezing January weather and earmuffs and great coats were in evidence on Baker Street. Holmes was up when I descended from our second story and the smell of his strong shag was everywhere in our sitting room. His manner was quite cherry as he rang for Mrs. Hudson and poured me a cup of coffee from the great silver urn.

"Come, Watson, we shall satisfy your inner man with that mainstay of the Empire, a stout English breakfast, and then be about our work. Duty beckons."

I was delighted since Holmes' statement indicated that I was to be a part of his investigation, not always the case though he did see to it that I was privy to the conclusion of most of his efforts.

It was not long afterwards that we were at the door of the modest home of the Dowager Countess of Parle, not far from Portman Square. To my surprise, it was the Countess herself who responded to our ring.

"Mr. Holmes, of course," she said immediately, in a rather grand manner that held no trace of condescension. "Surely this is Doctor Watson, whose writings I have enjoyed so much," she continued, indicating for us both to enter. As we muttered suitable greetings, the lady ushered us into her sitting room which was as neat as a pin though I noted few mementos of her husband's very old and distinguished family, nor of Lady Gertrude's either, she being of the Kerrs, a well known Devon family.

When we were seated, an aged retainer looking somewhat flustered appeared with the inevitable tea and crumpets. I noted the tea set bore the Parle crest and was faultlessly shiny. "Your note, Mr. Holmes," the Countess was saying, "explained the purpose of your visit. Cream, Doctor Watson?"

I responded in the negative.

"I have given all the information at my disposal to the authorities," she continued, "but can certainly go over it again."

Her face, rather heavily lined, relaxed in a winning smile. Her coiffure was bravely and carefully perfect as a gesture towards the inroads of time and her habiliments, somewhat dated in style, were immaculate.

"No doubt the insurance people have been here as well?" suggested Holmes.

A shadow crossed her face. "Actually, no. I am not of a practical nature and..." She waved a carefully tended hand in an aimless gesture.

"Then the studs were not insured." Holmes did not wait for an answer but pressed on. "A frequent oversight and one I come in contact with often."

"Actually, Mr. Holmes, it would..."

For some reason my friend did not seem disposed to let the Countess complete her sentence. "This situation is not as depressing as it might seem at first sight," he said hastily. "My associate and I have a good idea of who the thief is and..."

This time it was Holmes who was interrupted.

"Surely, sir, you cannot suspect my Matilda." Our hostess gestured with one expressive hand in the direction that the maid had departed.

"Certainly not," Holmes' voice was reassuring and soothing. "It is a professional thief, a foreigner in fact. The point is that he makes a habit of ridding himself of his spoils very promptly indeed, securing hard currency in exchange. If we are able to intercept the money given to the scoundrel by an associate, that will be a partial compensation for your loss."

The Countess seemed to have reservations. "But Mr. Holmes..."

"I do feel, Lady Gertrude, that the studs will be most difficult to locate. Therefore, Doctor Watson and I will attempt to secure the money paid for them by a fence."

"Pardon?" The Countess registered puzzlement, a fact that I could well recognize.

"A fence is a disposer of stolen goods," explained Holmes, rising from his chair. "Now we must get to work, Lady Gertrude. My thanks for your hospitality."

The sleuth was making for the front door quite abruptly, a fact that further bemused the Countess.

"But I didn't tell him anything about the robbery," she said.

Knowing the signs, I could respond with some authority.

"At this point, Mr. Holmes has all the facts he needs, Lady Gertrude."

When we re-entered our waiting Hansom, the driver handed Holmes an envelope.

"A street arab brung it, Mr. 'Olmes," he stated.

My friend tore open the message eagerly. "Wiggens found us, Watson. Invaluable, that young rascal. Ah-hah, what have we here?" He turned to me with a triumphant look. "It's from Gregson. VonSeddar, the Dutchman, was in London last night and has now disappeared."

"What does that mean?"

"The studs went with him. He's probably across the channel now by way of a private vessel hired for the job."

"Then, as you indicated to the Countess, it is best to forget the diamonds."

"Definitely." Holmes did not seem at all downcast by this turn of events, a reaction which I found surprising. "Now, Watson, we shall inquire into the matter of a knick-knack shop and one, Miss Mergatroid."

The establishment of the lady in question was on Vesely and I spied the Ponsbey Pub several blocks away. Miss Mergatroid was alone in her humble place of business and her eyes widened with surprise when Holmes introduced himself.

"Coo... 'ere's one fer the books. Mr. 'Olmes, hisself. 'T'is 'bout the Ponsbey raid last night, fer sure. The Peelers need some 'elp, eh sir?"

"Everyone needs help, Miss Mergatroid," replied Holmes. That statement certainly startled me, coming from him, so I put no credence in it. "What an interesting shop you have," he continued. "I note you specialize in Valentines."

"Quite a call fer 'em, sir," the woman responded in a matter of fact manner. "Ever since Kate Greenway painted hers, our English ones 'as 'ad a wide market."

"Good heavens, do you export them?"

"I gets orders from America, I does." was her proud reply.

"Why Miss Mergatroid, you must be competing with Ester Howland."

"My 'Olmes, you're joshing wiv me. The Yank, Howland, 'as a bleeding assembly line wot makes her stuff. I 'ear tell she's got a twenty thousand pound a year business and some of 'er cards fetch two quid."

"Amazing," replied Holmes with every indication of intense interest. I was in doubt as to his sincerity for he would have made a splendid actor. "Regarding the matter of the pub last night. Did you make note of another lady who was present? Possibly a stranger?"

"You must mean the one wot was in the potty ahead o' me."

I must say I winced at this frank declaration. Holmes responded with a nod and a smile.

"Didn't know the fluff, fer a fact. Kinda tall. 'Ad a nice hat, she did."

"What kind of coat?"

"Long, yuh know. Almost to 'er heels, it was. Never wear anything like that myself. Likes to 'ave a bit of me stems show."

Miss Mergatroid gestured towards her legs and I had to agree with her that they were shapely indeed.

"Well, our thanks," said Holmes to my surprise. He seemed to be making a habit of exits on this particular day.

When we returned to Baker Street, Billy the page boy informed us that Tobias Gregson was waiting in our chambers. Holmes had not been communicative during our return but he had hummed a sprightly air which indicated that he was well pleased with himself.

"Did you receive my message, Mr. Holmes?" asked the Scotland Yard Inspector as we entered our sitting room.

"Good show, that," replied Holmes, hanging up his Inverness. "Best to write off the Dutchman and the studs as well."

Gregson nodded in a gloomy manner. "By now the diamonds are in different settings no doubt."

"Of that, I'm not so sure," was my friend's cryptic response. "However, we can inscribe a finis to this matter and, as our American cousins might say 'pick up whatever marbles are left.'"

I must say this took the wind out of my sails and Gregson's eyes popped as well.

Holmes had his pipe in hand by now and had assumed a familiar stance by the mantle, a pose that had signified the end to many a previous adventure.

"First," he stated, rather smugly I thought, "the figure that disappeared into the Ponsbey Pub was Galantine, of course."

"What happened to him?" stammered Gregson.

"He walked out under your nose. You said the nighttime figure was caped. What you actually saw was a long woman's coat. The thief did not duck into the pub just to escape you. That was his predetermined destination after effecting the burglary. He was disguised as a woman. He made a beeline for the ladies' room to leave the jewels, probably in the cabinet of the water closet. That is his style you know, get rid of the loot immediately. Now we have Miss Mergatroid who followed him immediately into the toilet. She retrieved the gems. The Frenchman must have been rattled by your unexpected appearance for his sang froid deserted him. In giving a name to your assistant, Perkins, the best he could come up with was Gallant, the English translation of Galantine by the way."

Gregson was positively stunned and then his expression segued into abject embarrassment that was painful to see.

"Come now," said Holmes, "all is not lost. His associate, Miss Mergatroid got the money from VonSeddar and passed the studs on to him. All you have to do is have customs check for a package of Valentines which she will ship to America. Within the Valentines will be the payment due Galantine. You will give that money to the Dowager Countess I assume."

Gregson thought for a moment. "Yes, the Crown can't impound it and, though it is from an illegal source, Lady Gertrude would certainly have first call on it."

"You get your reward as well," stated Holmes. "The address on the package of Valentines will lead the American authorities to Galantine. You have but to extradite him and you've got your man."

"And Miss Mergatroid as well," exclaimed Gregson, full of sudden enthusiasm.

"The lady has been carefully schooled in her supposed business and I rather believe she's acted as a go-between on a number of matters for VonSeddar. You may solve more than one case through her. I fancy she has a record in the states."

"You mean she's an American?" I exclaimed.

"She played her part well, Watson, but words like potty

for toilet or stems for legs...? She's a colonial, you can be sure."

Gregson did not remain to hear any more discussion but was off to Scotland Yard, his eyes aglow.

I found myself excited as well. "I must say, Holmes, this is one of your most dazzling denouments. What a shame that the Countess has to lose her studs."

"Alas, Watson, she lost them long ago via various pawn shops." As I gazed at him with a slack jaw, his eyes twinkled.

"That is our real triumph, you see. The Lady Gertrude will receive a sizeable sum of money for nothing more than paste. Surely you noted the signs of financial stress. The one servant who probably has not received payment in months. There was no insurance because Lady Gertrude could not afford the premiums. She wanted to tell us the studs were ersatz but I couldn't allow that. She's held her head high, Watson, and perhaps we have helped her to continue to do so. At least, that is my hope."

The case did not wind down exactly as planned for Galantine remained at large. On February 14th, we received a plain envelope with no return address which told the whole story. The unsigned message within read as follows:

Monsieur Holmes: The idea...it should have worked. But then, poof, it evaporated in thin air. Only one man could have caused this so I address this message, with confidence, to Le Roi of the sleuths. Our paths will not cross again. I must remain on the other side of the ocean since the minons of the Dutchman are after me for passing paste.

The plan was sound, it was the perfect crime. Only you could have ruined my dream sublime. Mr. Holmes, don't be my Valentine.

"Well," said Holmes with a chuckle, "we must give the Frenchman credit for a sense of humor."

THE FRAIL SUSPECT

For the better part of a week storm, brewed in the witches cauldron of the Hebrides, had been driven south by the whiplash of high winds to unleash their violence over London. This particular night proved no exception. The banshee wailings of frigid gusts served as an eerie background for the tampini of tiny bullets of rain splattering against the glass of Baker Street windows. Without, all was wet and dank and cold but within the famous suite shared by Holmes and myself, the hearth fire radiated welcome warmth and created a cozy haven from the great elemental forces that buffeted the bastions of man.

Needless to say, I was much surprised when a wet and disheveled Inspector Alec MacDonald appeared at our door. The removal of his great coat, a seat by the fire and an extra tumbler from the sideboard erase the Scot's scowl but there was still considerable dissatisfaction on his rough hewn face as he toasted us and took a sizeable draft...for medicinal purposes of course.

Holmes' eyes twinkled as he regarded MacDonald.

"If we've driven the chill from your bones, ol' fellow,

possibly we can also relieve your inner stress. It is obvious your coming here tonight was no idle whim. A troublesome case, perhaps?"

"I wish I was sure," replied the Inspector. "T'is the matter of Malcolm Ramsey."

"The Art critic," stated Holmes promptly. "What problem involves him?"

"Ah then, you haven't heard. He was shot to death this very evening."

"Do tell," I exclaimed.

"No great surprise." Holmes comment was laconic. "The gentleman was not famous for his popularity. But as to his murder, and I assume it was that, do we face another case devoid of clues?"

"Few clues needed," said MacDonald somewhat bitterly. "We have but one suspect and what looks like an air-tight case. And yet...there's something about it that bothers me." He glanced at Holmes and then me, shamefaced.

"You'll make sport of me for saying it but the taste just isn't right."

Contrary to MacDonald's expectations, Holmes was gazing at him with added respect. "After a lengthy career in the field of criminology, it would be strange indeed if you did not possess a distinct feel for such matters. My congratulations Mr. Mac. Now do tell us what it is specifically that wrinkles your nose with doubt."

The Inspector shot a wary look at Holmes as if suspecting that he was being twitted but the great consulting detective was completely serious so the Aberdonian plunged into his tale.

"Ramsey's body was found by his butler at seven this evening in the upstairs study of his home on Belgrave Square. A bullet from an Adams .450 revolver had caught him right between the eyes and was lodged in his brain. Death was instantaneous of course."

"You established the make and calibre of the murder weapon with admirable promptness," commented Holmes.

"And without difficulty, since the gun was on the floor of the room." MacDonald exhibited a sly smile. "Before you ask, we did check the weapon for fingerprints and there were none."

"None at all or none that could be identified?"

"The gun had been wiped clean." At a nod from Holmes the Inspector continued. "Beside Ramsey, there were three other occupants of the house. Hernon, the butler, and his wife Matilda, who is cook-housekeeper. Also a Miss Vanessa Claremont who is Ramsey's ward."

Of a sudden, I snapped my fingers."Something has been nagging at me and now I have it. Miss Claremont is a patient of Doctor Goodbody. He has spoken to me of her."

"Fine fellow, Goodbody," said Holmes. Obviously his mind harkened back to the singular matter of "The Poison Plot" n which Doctor Goodbody was so very involved. Inasmuch as the Inspector was regarding me with considerable interest I felt prompted to continue.

"Miss Claremont is but twenty-three and suffers from pernicious anemia. Goodbody has her on a special diet highly fortified with liver but the case bothers him. She weighs but seven stone and is a frail reed indeed."

"I'm told that Ramsey did not treat the poor thing at all well. Perhaps that has colored my thinking. But let me conclude this strange tale," he said with a sigh. "Ramsey was not out of his house the entire day, no suprise considering the weather. The mansion itself has a bearing on the case. It contains art objects of considerable alue and is something of a fortress. Bars on all the windows and secure locks on stout doors. It was the habit of the household to make sure everything was bolted up come nightfall."

"Shortly after five this time of year." Holmes' eyes were dreamy with thought.

MacDonald nodded in agreement. "It was the sound of the firearm that alarmed the butler, Herndon. He came from the servants quarters on the run to find the ward, Vanessa Claremont on the stairs leading to the upstairs study. Her story was that she had been in her ground floor quarters when she had heard the shot and had started up instinctively ut had become frightened."

"Whereas she might have fired the gun and started down for all the butler knew," commented Holmes.

"Indeed, Sir. In any case, Herndon discovered the body and raced downstairs to summon a constable. Rushing by Miss Claremont, he shouted that the master was dead at which point she fainted. Fortunately, there was an officer close by on the Square and he returned with the butler. Herndon nd his wife revived Miss Claremone while the counstable notified the Yard and there you are."

The Inspector leaned back in his chair as if relieved to have gotten the main narrative out of the way. He well knew that pertinent questions would be asked.

Holmes was regarding the dancing flames in the hearth fire thoughtfully.

"You said there was but one suspect and a seemingly airtight case. Let me see. The house was securely locked two hours before the fatal shot. I assume that is confirmed by direct testimony."

MacDonald nodded. "As was the custom, Herndon checked all the doors and windows shortly after five. Miss Claremont confirms this since she was cleaning downstairs at the time." Since Holmes made no comment, the Inspector continued. "Actually Miss Claremont was little better than a maid in the establishment. She is the niece of Ramsey's deceased wife and the art critic took her in because of a proviso in Mrs. Ramsey's will. But he did not relish the arrangement and made no effort to conceal his feelings."

"No love lost between the two." Holmes mused for a moment. "I assume the shot fired at seven, which alerted the household, was the one that killed Ramsey."

"We had a pathalogist on the scene in short order," replied the Inspector. "Just as a matter of procedure since the corpse was still bleeding when the constable got there. Remsey was shot at seven, for a fact."

"With three people on the scene,"stated Holmes, "your prime suspect is obviously the ward, Vanessa Claremont. Motive must point the finger of guild."

"Indeed, Sir. Neither Harndon, the butler, nor his wife had reason to wish their master dead. On the other hand, Miss Claremont stands to inherit Ramsey's considerable estate. If she evades the gallows for his murder, that is." The Scot was shaking his head.

"The ward had both motive and opportunity but you are still dissatisfied?"

"Aye, Sir. T'is the feel."

"With which I agree completely," was Sherlock Holmes suprising response.

I rose from my chair with a groan. "So it's off to the scene of the crime, is it? I could wish murders would occur during more clement weather."

My confrere chuckled. "Do resume your seat, ol' fellow, unless you wish to replenish Mr. Mac's glass. I have no intention of going forth on this night. Rather we shall solve the problem in comfortable surroundings."

"Will you now?" MacDonald seemed ruffled but his manner mellowed when I brought him a refill along with a cigar.

"More questions of course," stated Holmes," though I've already conceived the solution, in part. Malcolm Ramsey was a busy man and since he did not stray from his domicile during the day, I assume there were visitors."

"Three." The inspector referred to his official notebook. "At two in the afternoon his business manager, Ezra Hinshaw, consulated with him regarding a series of lectures at local art groups. He brought contracts for the engagements which were duly signed and witnessed by Herndon. He then departed. At three, a Vicar Bisbee arrived in hopes of securing a donation for a local charity. Whether Ramsey complied or not I have not learned but the Vicar's reputation in these parts is well known. He is somewhat deaf and very near sighted."

"We can rule Bisbee out for obvious reasons," remarked Holmes.

Aside from the Vicar's line of work I could divine no obvious reasons but I withheld comment on the matter.

"Shortly after five, one Cedric Folks visited Ramsey. Bit of a neer-do-well, that one. Orbits 'round the edge of society as a painter of sorts. Attended Sandhurst but left under something of a cloud. Haven't run him down yet but evidentally his visit to Ramsey was connected with the art world. He left shortly after five, slamming the front door forceably. This sound brought the butler into the hall. Ramsey appeared at the head of the stairs and directed the servant to secure the doors carefully. Herndon told me that Ramsey appeared angry. It was the last time he saw the art critic alive,"

"Did the butler make any other comment about this incident?" McDonald's brow furrowed in thought. "Simply that he went through his usual procedure of shooting the bolts on the front door and then checking the windows."

"Wait a bit," the inspector added. "He did say he heard the horses hooves outside and saw the hansom that Folks came in depart."

Holmes rubbed his hands with what I recognized as a gesture of satisfaction. "Now, as the butler went about his regular task I presume that Ramsey returned to his upstairs study?"

"Yes, Sir. As the butler completed his security tour, Miss Claremont went to her room on the ground floor. She engaged in needle work but her door was open. She stated that neither Herndon nor his wife come from the servant quarters before the shot was fired. Because of the layout of the house, they would have had to pass her door."

All this was intriguing me."The prime suspect gives the servants a fool proof alibi? She might better have kept silent about the matter."

"Uncontestable alibis frequently arouse my suspicions," remarked Holmes. "Though in this case I agree witn you, Watson. But it is of no matter since I have learned what I wish to know. Gentlemen, a prima facie case for your consideration."

Knowing my confrere so well, I recognized the signs.

The very manner in which Holmes leaned back in his chair told the story. Gone was the hawk-like, almost preditory manner of the great man-hunter hot on the scent. Instead there was the calm theorist of Baker Street, ready with his trademarked tour de force.

"Daily study of the journals makes one privy to seemingly odd incidents which prove helpful in filling out the pattern of puzzlemeiit. This final visitor of Ramsey, Cedric Folks, is attempting a career in art and had a showing recently. In covering the event, Ramsey stated in print that the painter was obviously trying to emulate the French impressionalist, Pissarro, but that his paintings created naught but a false impression. This acid critique elicited much ribald laughter in art circles and Folks, I must assume, became livid with rage. Recall his stormy departure from the art critic. You did mention that he slammed the outer door loudly."

The Scot, his eyes intent on Holmes, nodded briefly. "Now, Mr.Mac., regarding the upstairs study where Ramsey met his end. It is sizeable?"

"More than thirty feet in length."

"And the door to the study is adjacent to the staircase?"

"How did you know that?"

"To fit my reconstruction, it had to be."

I thought Holmes' smile was somewhat smug but quelled the thought being on tenter hooks for the denouement. Holmes resumed his summation. "Three inmates of the establishment and three visitors during the day. The deceassed's business manager and the Vicar can be ruled out, surely, for complete lack of motive, not to mention means. But Cedric Folks, the irate artist, had plenty of motive. Of the inmates, the servants are given an alibi by Vanessa Claremont. She had motive whereas they did not. However, the lady, because of the crime itself, certainly has an alibi."

"If she does, I canna' see it."

"Come now, a frail young woman shoots Ramsey with a .450 Adams revolver? I'm in doubt if she could even manage the trigger pull of such a heavy calibre weapon. But to expect her to fire it with marksmanship accuracy over a distance of thirty feet is asking the impossible."

"Could she not have been close to Ramsey when she shot him?" MacDonald was far from convinced.

"Had Miss Claremont been close to the victim, the bullet would have torn through his head and imbedded itself in the wall. You said it was lodged in his brain. Come, come, Inspector; we are speaking of a heavy piece of ordinance with a high muzzle velocity."

MacDonald shot a sheepish look at me. "He's right, you know," was his grudging admission.

"He usually is," I replied.

"I ruled out your prime suspect promptly," continued Holmes. "When Cedric Folks rushed down the stairs shortly after five in the evening, he opened the front door and then slammed it shut without leaving the house. Instead, he immediately concealed himself within. Behind a convenient sofa, perhaps. The butler, thinking he had left, locked up the house. Outside there was the sound of the departing hansom. When the time seemed right, Folks stole up the stairs, opened the door to the study and, as Ramsey turned at the sound, he fired from the doorway. He did attent Sandhurst you said. I'll wager you'll discover that he is an excellent shot. Wiping the gun clean, he threw it into the murder room and raced down the stairs again to hide below. The body was discovered, the butler rushed outside and Miss Claremont fainted. At this point, Folks escaped from the house unnoticed though he might have done so later when the patrolman arrived and all attention was directed to the upstairs study where the victim's body lay. There's your case for you, MacDonald, all tied up neatly. And the resolution did not require Watson's braving the elements after all."

The Inspector was shaking his head. "I've a thought that I'm going to look like a fool but there's one wee matter, Mr. Holmes. If Folks did not leave the house, how was it that the hansom that brought him departed?"

"But that's the whole key to the matter. I could well reconstruct what happened but how could you prove it in count? Folks hired the conveyance and instructed the driver to leave when he slammed the front door. He gave the man a sizeable fee, no doubt. The hansom driver is the tool to force a confession from Folks. Just locate him and you have your witness to the fact that the artist did not, in reality, leave the Ramsey mansion at five o'clock."

It was after a grim but satisfied Inspector MacDonald left that Holmes had a final comment.

"You know, my dear Watson, at first glance this matter seemed bizarre indeed. An outre affair. But it was all quite simple, really."

"Elementary, my dear Holmes." was my dry rejoinded.

THE PURLOINED PEARLS

It was a blustery autumnal day that found me descending from my bedchamber at a late hour. Sherlock Holmes' life style was quite as bohemian as mine but somehow he always seemed to be up and about before me. Of course, there were those times that he never went to bed.

I found my friend seated at the breakfast table over a final cup of coffee, regarding a letter. The smell of the strong shag he fancied permeated the room.

"Here's something that shows promise, my good Watson," he said, passing the single sheet of stationery to me. The message was machine written and had the grace of brevity.

"Dear Mr. Holmes,
      I am beset with a problem which demands your talents. A crime can be prevented if only I can secure your assistance. I will be at your chambers at eleven this morning with the sincere hope that you will be present and will grant me an audience.
      Fred Alibright."

"It seems no more than the usual plea for aid," I stated.

Holmes' eyebrows escalated. "Come, come, ol' friend. You are well aware that most of our cases relate to crimes committed or a strong suspicion of the fact. Our clients require solutions or retribution. Here, we are told that no criminal act has been committed. I have long contended that doctors should be more involved in preventative medicine. Possibly we can be instrumental in some preventative deduction, hence the matter suggests interesting overtones."

Not long thereafter, the first sound of the church bells were striking the hour. Holmes' keen eyes rose from some clippings he was studying and his thin face turned towards the outer door of the famous chambers at 221B Baker Street.

"I fancy Mr. Allbright is approaching the landing now, Watson," he stated. After a crisp knock and a call to enter from Holmes, the door opened to prove that the sleuth, as usual, was quite right.

Fred Allbright was of moderate height with shoulders of respectable proportions, the beginnings of a paunch and a receding hair line. His face was of good color with broad features. He wore a checkered suit that could not be considered conservative by the most lenient of critics. His manner was friendly but more expansive than seemed proper for an English gentleman. This matter was solved by his opening words.

"Gee, this is sure a pleasure, Mr. Holmes. Even in the states your name cuts a wide furrow. This here must be Doctor Watson," he continued, relinquishing Holmes' hand and capturing mine.

"Quite," I responded, somewhat at a loss for words.

"Fer a fact," was the man's answer as he sank into an easy chair, indicated by the detective. "I am a troubleshooter, Sir. An elastic occupation since my assignments might involve anything. In any case, I had a bit of a windfall several years back. I had done some work for Cyrus Muldoon, the cereal king."

Since Allbright paused, for no obvious reason, Holmes offered a comment.

"Muldoon Munchies, the breakfast food of American youth."

"That's the sales slogan, Mr. Holmes, Old Cyrus' son got in a couple of scrapes and he hired me to smooth things over. One day I suggested an idea to Cyrus and he went for it like a ton of brick. 'Ideas save time and time is money,' is a maxim of his."

"Not without merit," said Holmes with a suggestive glance at his watch.

"Forgive me but the background is necessary. I suggested a premium in every box of Muldoon Munchies. A small photograph of a baseball star. Muldoon seized upon it and before you could shake a stick there was pictures of Joseph Jackson, George Herman Ruth and Grover Cleveland Alexander by the bushel load. Kids all over the states thought it was the cat's whiskers."

"I sense this matter will intrigue me, Mr. Alibright," said Holmes rising to his feet. "I have a luncheon scheduled with Doctor Watson's brother. If you will pardon me for a moment, I shall dispatch our page boy to cancel the engagement and devote my full time to your difficulty."

"Gee, Mr. Holmes, that's great," said Alibright with gusto. Holmes rang for Billy and confered with the boy on the stair landing while I tried to mask my astonishment. My brother had been dead for some years and I realized that Holmes' remark was a patent falsehood though for what reason the great sleuth wished to speak to Billy, I could not fathom.

"Please continue," said Holmes, returning to his chair as the page boy flew down the stairs on some errand.

"Well, Mr. Holmes, old Cyrus figured I was a pretty sharp

article so when he allowed the Van Syckle necklace to be shipped over here for the exhibition at the British Museum, he sent me along to keep tabes on it."

"Don't tell me it has been stolen!"

"No but it will be, sure as the moon ain't blue cheese."

I was entranced. The Van Syckle pearl necklace was well known indeed and I recalled that Holmes had mentioned that the strand of matched pearls had changed hands recently and for a breathtaking price.

"I never figured the pearls was in any danger," continued Allbright, "what with the security measures at the Museum and all that. But one gets to know a wide circle in my field and I ran into a chap over here that I'd met in the states. He owed me something so he tipped me off that a continental gang of jewel thieves had their sights set on the pearls. Well, I got right on my hobby horse and checked the thing out. It's that Deuxieme Sept crowd from Paris, Mr. Holmes. They are headquartered at the Wheatley Tavern in Tyrell's Wood. I understand they've secured a duplicate of the necklace that's so good it would fool Muldoon himself or any expert that wasn't suspicious of a switch. Now here's the way I figure this. Whatever the Deuxieme Sept mob figure on pulling depends on the substitute necklace. Without that they won't have time to act before the exhibition is over and I'm headed back to old New York with the genuine article."

Holmes' aquiline face had been directed towards the flickering flames of the hearthfire but he now turned towards his visitor with an expression of approval. "An acute observation, that. Do I sense you are thinking of purloining the pearls?"

"The fake ones, Mr. Holmes, fer a fact. I have no idea where to look fer them but a man of your experience could certainly figure out where the mob has them hidden."

"Good heavens!" I interjected, "you are proposing robbery and Holmes would be facing a whole gang of French ruffians."

"Would I not have you to aid me, old comrade?" said the sleuth, his eyes twinkling.

"If necessary," I stammered. "But why doesn't Mr. Allbright go to the police and the museum officials with his story?"

"They'd never take me seriously Doctor. No crime has been committed and the Deuxieme Sept gang couldn't be arrested for having a string of fake pearls even if I could prove that Van Seddar of Amsterdam created them. Oh, I might cause a little stir but they'd just put an extra guard on duty and write it off as a nervous American. I happen to know the gang is coming to London tomorrow night. That's probably when they figure to steal the pearls and substitute the fakes so you'll have to work fast, Mr. Holmes. I'll keep my eye on the Frenchmen and come back here tomorrow night. I'm prepared to offer two thousand pounds for the fake necklace."

I must have looked startled and Allbright indulged in a dry chuckle. "I'll take them back to old Cyrus and persuade him to have his wife wear the erzatz necklace at social functions while the real thing remains in a bank vault. It's the kind of idea that will appeal to him and he'll shell out your fee for the duplicate, have no fear."

"But," said Holmes, "you will pay the money prior to leaving for America?"

"Certainly. If you secure the fakes by tomorrow night, I'll have the two thousand quid ready." Allbright lapsed into silence, regarding Holmes with anxious eyes. The great detective seemed to come to a decision.

"I do have an interest in oddments of this sort."

I was thunderstruck. "But Holmes, the risk?"

"He who never takes a risk accomplishes little," replied my friend, somewhat pontifically, but there was a warning glitter in his cold eyes that caused me to suppress other objections to this fool's errand.

Alibright was delighted. "That's great, Mr. Holmes. I figure the gang will be in London about six tomorrow night. I'll keep my eye on them and then meet you back here later."

He gathered his coat and hat with a satisfied air. During goodbyes, I could scarce contain myself wondering why Holmes would associate himself with what could only be described as a second story job.

As the door closed on our visitor, Holmes signalled for me to remain silent while he listened to the receding footsteps. He then swiftly crossed to the corner window signalling for me to join him. Concealed by the drapes, Baker Streets most illustrious resident watched the exterior of Mrs. Hudson's establishment. Alibright appeared in but a moment and made off down the street. From a doorway there materialized a slight, dark man who seemed to direct a signal towards us as he sauntered after the Commission Agent.

"Slippery Styles," said Holmes by way of explanation. "The human shadow as he is sometimes called and he deserves the title. I had Billy fetch him when it became apparent that Mr. Allbright warranted our close attention."

"Holmes, I am completely befuddled. Why did you agree to help the American forstall a jewel robbery?"

The great sleuth regarded me with a resigned air. "Fred Allbright is about as American as you are, Watson. Did it not strike you that his attempt at the idiom and mannerisms of a colonial smacked of a music hall entertainer? In the parlance of the theatre, Allbright's performance was more suited to vaudeville than the legitimate stage. Recall his idea for a premium which supposedly captured the fancy of Cyrus Muldoon."

"Not a bad thought," said I, defensively.

"But he mentioned Joseph Jackson. No American would call the outfielder anything but Joe Jackson and more probably Shoeless Joe Jackson as he is affectionately known by his countrymen. Also, an American would certainly say Babe Ruth rather than George Herman Ruth. I doubt if half of his millions of fans even know his given name. Those were but a few of Allbright's errors. He mentioned two thousand pounds and, but a moment later, said 'two thousand quid.' His idea is inventive but his execution leaves much to be desired."

"Then his whole story is a fabrication?"

"Oh, no. The plot to secure the Van Syckle necklace is

genuine, I'm sure. He just misled us as regards the time table. Now I must pack an overnight bag and be off. Do cable the Wheatley Tavern in Tyrell's Wood and reserve a room for Captain Simesby Froylott, ol' chap."

I brightened, "I'll be ready in a trice." Though as confused as before, the prospect of the game being afoot always stimulated me.

"No, good fellow, your presence is needed here. A message will arrive no doubt from Slippery Styles relating the whereabouts and activities of our larcenous client. Have Billy run it to Lestrade's office at the Yard."

Shortly thereafter, Holmes, disguised as a grizzled sea captain, departed.

The great detective did not return till early evening the following day. His self satisfied air prompted me to hazard a guess.

"You got the necklace!"

"It was amazingly easy." Occasionally Holmes attempted to assume the mantle of modesty but on his restless shoulders it proved an ill fitting garment. "I managed to secure a room adjacent to the suite in the Tavern occupied by a group of Frenchmen. While they were at dinner, I was able to bore a hole through the wainscoting of their sitting room."

"A peephole," I exclaimed.

"Exactly. Later I activated the Tavern's fire alarm. Quite naturally the thieves secured the necklace from its hiding place and returned it when they realized there had been a false alarm."

"With you watching them."

"The Deuxieme Sept people will be in London by now and I fancy we shall hear from Lestrade at any moment."

"But won't the gang be panicked at losing their bogus necklace?"

"They won't realize anything is amiss since I left another necklace in their hiding place."

"But why..." I began, only to stop at a gesture by Holmes.

"Patience, good fellow, I hear Lestrade's footfalls on our stairs and he has questions that require answering as well."

Holmes had the door open before the Scotland Yard Inspector

reached the landing and ushered the lean and ferret-like detective within.

"I trust you have good news?" Evidentally Lestrade did since his face was flushed with excitement and satisfaction.

"It was a lovely sight, I'll tell you. When we burst into the room, there was Guy Spaull with the pearls in his hand. He knew he'd had it and when I snapped the cuffs on him, he made only one comment. He looked me in the eyes, he did, and said: 'I'll wager Holmes had a hand in this.'"

"Did he now," exclaimed the sleuth. Appreciation of his talent was always welcome, regardless of the source. "So you got them all."

"Except the guard. He was by a window when we burst in and jumped, eluding my men on the street below. But we'll get him."

"Possibly sooner than you think."

"Here's that false necklace you requested," continued Lestrade, "though I can't figure why you want it."

"The counterfeit might prove useful," replied Holmes laconically. I waited for the great sleuth to stand in his oft used position by the mantlepiece, a signal that his summation was to be delivered. Holmes did not disappoint me.

"From the start I believed that the Van Syckle necklace was the target of thieves. Alibright's knowledge of the plot was in such detail that he had to be part of the conspiracy. He wanted to...I believe the expression is... 'to pick up all the marbles.'"

Holmes' sparkling eyes centered on me. "Yesterday, before going to Tyrell's Wood, I contacted Lestrade and, after some persuasion, took him to the British Museum where we were able to establish that the necklace on display was false."

"Then it had already been stolen," I said.

"Allbright is one of the guards at the Museum, a key man in the substitution, but he did not plan it. Nor did the Deuxieme Sept gang. They were all but hired assistants, mercenaries of crime."

"You figured it for a Guy Spaull mme caper," said

Lestrade.

"It had his mark on it," was Holmes' response. (See *"The Double Deception"*) "After the substitution was effected, the conspirators laid low to see if there was any hue and cry and to arrange to transport the necklace to the Continent. I realized that their meeting tonight was for the payoff."

"Payoff?" I echoed.

"Spaull was to take possession of the necklace and pay his hirelings their agreed wages. Allbright, as one of those involved, had to be present though he was in hopes that I had already secured the real necklace. As soon as I learned, via Slippery Styles, that Allbright had gone to The Archery Tavern to what seemed to be a private party, I notified Lestrade and he descended on the place with a flying squad. Allbright must have been surprised when the French thieves showed up with a necklace. He realized that there had been a new development which, no doubt, explains why he was positioned by a window ready to escape if necessary."

Some light was dawning in my mind. "Then Allbright was attempting to use you to doublecross his associates."

"Correct. We could have arrested the gang in Tyrell's Wood and Alibright as well. But I wanted to capture Reggie Bonhomme. He has eluded me for too long."

Suddenly the great detective's form stiffened.

"Quick, Lestrade, get into the next room. We are about to have a visitor." As the Inspector disappeared, Holmes continued softly. "Do you have your pistol available, Watson?"

"The desk drawer," I responded automatically.

"Do secure it and have it ready in your pocket."

There was a rapid tattoo on the outer door and Holmes crossed to open it. Fred Alibright looked disheveled as he entered but he still possessed his genial manner.

"Evening, Mr. Holmes. Were you able to secure the counterfeit pearls?"

"I was," replied the sleuth. Allbright's eyes widened with surprise for a moment. "As regards the agreed fee..." continued

Holmes.

Allbright looked chagrined. "I was only able to secure a thousand pounds on such short notice. Would you accept that along with my marker for the rest?"

"I find that arrangement satisfactory."

The self-styled Commission Agent hastily thrust a bundle of currency into Holmes' hands and rapidly scribbled an I.O.U. which he left on the desk as the sleuth handed him the substitute necklace. Obviously the man felt that defeat had turned to victory but, as he inspected the pearls a cloud passed over his round face.

"What's this? There's something off center here."

"I think not," said Holmes quietly. "I agreed to secure the imitation pearls for you and you have them."

The veins in Allbright's forehead stood out and he regarded Holmes malevolently. As his hand stole towards his hip pocket, I brought my revolver into view and the menace in Alibright's manner evaporated.

"You've been on to me right along," he managed to say in a hoarse voice.

"Indeed," replied Holmes as he summoned Lestrade from the adjacent room. While the Inspector handcuffed the dazed criminal, Holmes chose to be generous.

"Allbright, I'm going to do you a favor. Certain facts about this case will not be released to the press."

"How's that going to help me?" The question had a pitiful sound to it.

"Your associates will not discover that you were the clue that led to their incarceration. That fact should assure you a longer life span than you might otherwise expect."

Reggie Bonhomme and his mercenaries all went to penal institutions and were removed from society for some years. However, there was one final surprise which I considered most intriguing. Some two years later, Holmes received a package. On opening it he found one thousand pounds and a brief note.

"Dear Mr. Holmes:

Would you kindly destroy the marker in my name on receipt of this sum.

Fred Allbright"

THE SOCIETY THIEVES

It was a mild day in late Spring and Sherlock Holmes and I had attended a symphonic concert. The works of Handle and Bach were not exactly my cup of tea but I was always delighted to accompany Holmes to a musical event. Invariably he was able to lose himself on such occasions and his overly-active mind was diverted from the awesome schedule of his work.

That evening, after an excellent repast served by Mrs. Hudson, Holmes and I settled down for a quiet time. The sleuth occupied himself with a letter to Monsieur Dubugue of the Paris police, clearing up some matters relative to "The Case of the Mysterious Imprint," a matter which he had resolved and which earned him the undying gratitude of the Surete Francaise (see *Sherlock Holmes And The Panamanian Girls*). Since I had made that case history available to the reading public, I was going over some notes on the adventure in a reminiscent mood when our dedicated landlady reappeared at our door to announce the prescence of Inspector Stanley Hopkins downstairs. Holmes had the youthful policeman shown up at once for he had high hopes for Hopkins. Indeed, it was Holmes' influence that had been largely instrumental in Hopkins' transferral from the Down Country police to Scotland Yard where he was, already, beginning to make a name for himself.

I escorted our visitor in his quiet tweed suit to the armchair by the fire and made myself busy at the tantalus with a decanter and the gasogene.

Holmes, standing by the mantle stuffing shag into his cherrywood, surveyed his alert protoge with approving eyes.

"I sense an interesting puzzle, Hopkins, for we seldom see you unless the matter has tantalizing overtones. Wouldn't be about the rash of burglaries in fashionable areas, would it?"

"It's murder, Sir," stated Hopkins in his direct manner.

"Simon Sand, the bookmaker?"

"Right on, Mr. Holmes."

"Bludgeoned to death in Rolland Park, adjacent to his residence according to the journals."

"The information given to the press was brief and incomplete," said Hopkins, accepting the glass I handed him.

An additional spark of interest ignited Holmes' eyes.

"There was no suggestion of motive in the newsprint accounts though Sand's occupation would not excite a life insurance salesman to solicit his business."

"Agreed," stated Hopkins. "Sand was successful but had none of his profits in his possession when he left his office to dine at the Pall Mall Club. He spent a rather full evening there and the doorman secured a carriage for him at eleven last night which he directed, in somewhat slurred words, to the Kensington Arms."

"His apartment house," said Holmes. "Would he, by chance, have stopped the carriage by the park to seek the sobering effects of the night air?"

"No, Sir, and here's where the tantalizing overtones come in. We've located the driver and he tells an interesting tale. When he drew up at the Kensington Arms, he had to help Sand out of the vehicle for the man was considerably the worse for wear. The porter had taken the lift to the fifth floor but this was no problem since Sand's apartment was on the first floor. The bookmaker was without change and bade the driver wait for him while he secured the fare from his rooms. He seemed to negotiate the stairs without trouble and the porter heard Sand let himself into his chambers. When the porter came down, he found the driver waiting but his presence was easily explained and the two men conversed for about ten minutes. Knowing Sand's habits, the porter finally assumed that the bookmaker had passed out and it was he who paid the driver. For the rest of the night the porter was up and down in the lift several times but he kept his eye on Sand's apartment through the open grille on the first floor. He is firm in the conviction that the man could not have left the premises without his knowing of it."

"No back entry available?" I asked, sipping on my drink.

"None, doctor," replied Hopkins shaking his head.

"And yet," said Holmes, rather savoring his words, "early this morning a patrolling policeman found Sand's dead body on a bench in Rolland Park. Next to a clump of rhododendrons as I recall, though I cannot see how that fact is of any significance."

Holmes had seated himself and was gazing into the flickering flames of the hearthfire. Hopkins, who knew his habits and was a devoted admirer of the scientific methods of the famous amateur detective, preserved his silence. I knew Holmes' method better than the young Inspector and did likewise but I sensed that it was Holmes' uncanny ratiocination that would tear aside the veil of mystery. For once, I was proven right.

Finally Holmes spoke in that preoccupied manner that indicated he was marshalling all the facts at his disposal for a final review.

"Here we have a seeming impossibility which, as is so often the case, should make the solution all the more simple. Sand lets himself into his rooms, his condition such that we could expect him to sink into the nearest available chair and fall into an alcoholic sleep. How is the unconscious man transported into the park across from his residence? The porter says he kept his eye on Sand's apartment and he could not have left without being seen. He could be wrong but it is not likely since someone would have had to get into the apartment and carry Sand's body out of the building, a feat certainly to be observed. Of course, the inert body could have been lowered by rope from a back window but that would have been most chancy in that neighborhood, even in the dark hours of the night."

"There is an added complexity, Sir," stated Hopkins. "Sand had the only key to his rooms. Considering his profession, he must have had large sums of money on the premises from time to time and he took no chances. There was a specially designed Mills-Stroffner lock on the front door to his chambers that only his key could open."

As Holmes began to phrase a question, Hopkins anticipated him.

"We had Wells, from the Special Branch, take a look at the lock. It was not tampered with."

"I'll accept Well's opinion without question," said Holmes, musingly. "Happily it gives us the answer to the matter or I'm sadly mistaken.' The sleuth rose with gusto and there was that keen look about his predatory features.

"Hopkins, if you would drop by in the late morning, I do believe I'll have some news for you."

The Inspector's face registered disappointment but he knew his man, as did I. Holmes would reveal nothing until he "tidied up a few strands of loose yarn," as he sometimes put it.

After showing Stanley Hopkins out and exchanging a shrug of exasperation with him, I made ready to mount the back stairs to my bedchamber. For all I knew, Holmes might be out the whole night making contact with the many sources of information at his disposal. Certainly in the half-world of the lawless, my friend's lines of information were second to none. I was quite surprised when he bade me a cheery goodnight and made his way to his bed as well. Evidentally his inquiries were to await the morning sun.

It was eleven when an anxious Stanley Hopkins made his way to our door. I had arisen somewhat late and had not been surprised to learn that Holmes had already breakfasted and departed. Hopkins and I exchanged small talk over coffee and in a short while we were joined by the greatest deductive mind the world has ever known. There was that barely concealed look of smugness that invariably irritated me, being a reminder of my mental limitations.

Doffing his light coat and topper, the sleuth poured himself a cup of coffee, talking all the while which was not his custom.

"I'd best be brief, Hopkins," he said, "for you must be gone to get your cuffs on the murderer of Simon Sand. You'd also best see if that forensic genius, Spillsbury, can give you a fairly close approximation of the time of death. As for the solution, the facts lead us to the one possible answer. Sand had the only key to his rooms. It was impossible for him to leave the apartment unobserved and get to the park where he was found. Therefore he was never in his chambers. The driver, whom you know as Slocum, killed the bookmaker before taking him to the Kensington Arms. He waited till the porter went up in the lift and, using Sand's key, opened the door to the first floor chambers and then made his way down the stairs to await the return of the porter. He had already gotten rid of the body in the park though, after completing his fabrication with the porter, he had to return there to leave the key in the corpse's pocket."

His face wreathed with smiles, Hopkins rose as though to go but was forestalled.

"Not so fast. You are not after the driver, Slocum, but the gambler, Ned Rance. Rance arranged to use Slocum's carriage and name because he was into Sand's book for a large amount of money. The same can be said for three or four other London bookmakers. There were threats of bodily harm or worse unless he paid off. When Sand left his office, he was not carrying any large sum of currency but he was when he finally departed from the Pall Mall Club. There was the recent running of the Travers Stakes and a number of members of that less than sedate private establishment-I should not honor it with the word club-wagered heavily with Sand on the favorite, a disappointing fifth if you recall. Rance positioned himself with his borrowed carriage outside the club and made sure that it was he who picked up the inebriated bookmaker. The real Slocum, when he realizes what has happened, will be your best witness against Rance. In addition, said gambler has been spending the morning paying off his losses all over town. I don't believe the Prosecutor for the Crown will have much trouble with the case, Hopkins."

It was after the Inspector's departure that Holmes surveyed me with a wise smile. "I do believe I've come upon something, Watson."

"I know, I know," I groaned. "It's so simple after you explain it."

"Oh, the trifling matter of the Sand murder was not on my mind at all. Did I not make mention of the rash of society burglaries recently?"

"The papers are full of it."

"All right, what are the ingredients of a successful burglary?"

"An effective means of entry and egress, of course."

"Without doubt, but you have not gone far enough. Getting in and out of a residence when the inmates are not on the premises increases the possibility of success considerably since there is much less chance of detection."

"What are you getting at, Holmes?"

"An idea incubated by the Sand murder. Suppose a burglar was working in conjunction with some hansom and carriage drivers who concentrated their action in fashionable areas. When said drivers take a fare to a restaurant or, perhaps, a party or ball, they notify the swagman who can approach the residence without fear of arousing the owners. That is a little bee that I'll plant in Lestrade's bonnet. He's had some failures of late and needs a leg up."

It was not long after this discussion that Lestrade did get the credit for capturing what became known as "The Society Thieves."

It was during this period that New Scotland Yard gained its reputation as the foremost criminal investigation apparatus in the world. But I wonder how well the ferret-like Lestrade, the canny Scot, Alec MacDonald, the youthful Stanley Hopkins and their like would have done without the great amateur, the world's only Consulting Detective, Sherlock Holmes?

HALF A ROBBERY

I recall with great clarity when this matter came knocking on the door of 221B Baker Street since it marked a singular event. Indirectly, and for the first time in Sherlock Holmes' long career, Mrs. Hudson, our devoted landlady, contributed to Holmes' investigation of criminal activities.

It was a chilly winter morning shortly after we had finished a late breakfast. As was his frequent habit, Holmes was gazing out of the windows of the untidy flat at the street below. Apparently there was something of interest since, after a period of time, he summoned me to join him at his vantage point.

"Unless I am greatly misled," he said, "we shall soon have a visitor."

Following my friend's gaze, I observed a large woman on the pavement below who gave every indication of great indecision. Her hat was of the type that would be termed somewhat out of the fashion of the times. She was warmly clad, as befitted the weather, and the fur on her collar was of value. In size, she would have been termed 'formidable,' even by a casual observer.

Several times she made as if to cross the thoroughfare towards the downstairs door of our lodgings and then drew back as though in fear of what her actions would provoke. Finally, with a deep breath, she forced herself to cross the street and as we kept watch, she rang the bell of the house owned by Mrs. Hudson which had become so famous because of the tenant within.

It was but a short time before a tap on the door announced the arrival of Mrs. Hudson, followed by the lady Holmes had noticed on the street. For many years, Mrs. Hudson had seen a large contingent representing the law and an equally large group of the lawless pass through her portals. However, either by a quirk of her nature or a rigid self-discipline, she had adopted an attitude of obliviousness to the strange goings-on at her domicile. As a result, her manner was quite tentative as she addressed us.

"Mr. Holmes, sir, Dr. Watson, this is my friend, Florence Carstair, who's had a mite of trouble. I took the liberty of suggesting that she have a word with you about it."

"Why, of course, Mrs. Hudson," replied Holmes, with a warmth rather unusual for him. He ushered the nervous Florence Carstair towards a chair as Mrs. Hudson hovered by the door.

I offered my chair to our landlady who declined with firmness.

"I well knows that Mr. Holmes likes to get facts first hand, thank you. I has no association with the happening and if you will excuse me, I'll get some tea going right away." Turning to her friend, she said: "Florence, after you've had your little say to Mr. Holmes and the doctor here, why don't you come down to the kitchen for tea and scones?"

The amenities concluded, Mrs. Hudson fled.

As I assisted our visitor out of her considerable coat, made unnecessary by the cheery fire crackling in the hearth, the detective regarded her with a reassuring smile but there was a tinge of concern in his voice.

"Miss Carstair, the people who choose to have little chats with me almost always bring difficulties, problems, sometimes disasters, with them as companions. May I hope that your problem does not involve the Carstair pearls?"

Now seated, Florence Carstair regarded the detective with amazement.

"I'm quite familiar with your uncanny deductions, Mr. Holmes, but how could you possibly...?"

With a gentle wave of his hand, Holmes interrupted her question.

"Nothing revealing in your clothes or hands, which are so often a source of clues. In your case, the trained eye which I so delight in using merely read with great interest an article by Dr. Krenstroff, the famous German gem expert. The subject matter was the fabulous pair of black pearls which a sea captain named Andrew Carstair brought back from one of his voyages to the Orient. While the name, Carstair, is not an uncommon one, a hunch prompted me to assume that you could be Captain Carstair's daughter and the owner of the matched pearls."

"That's absolutely correct, Mr. Holmes," corroborated our visitor, "and it is about the pearls, or at least one of them, that I'm here today." As she warmed to her tale, the hesitant manner disappeared. "I live in the house my father left me on Horsham Square. Last night, quite late, I went into the study, which had been my father's favorite room, looking for a book. I found a man there and the safe in the wall was open. Without even thinking, I seized the poker by the fireplace and made for him. However, he was half-way to the French doors when I came into the room and he just raced out into the garden and the night."

The tale ended momentarily at this point as if the recounting of our visitor's bit of melodrama had been a wearing task indeed. She paused to mop her face with a wisp of cambric. Having followed her words avidly, I concluded that the sight of the ample Miss Carstair wielding a poker would have sent me to my heels as well, and as rapidly.

"I tried to take after him, gentlemen," continued Florence

Carstair, "but he was a fast one and over the garden wall before I got outside. Naturally my first thought was the pearls, so I returned to the safe. The case that my father always kept the black pearls in was open and one of them was gone."

"Only one?" Holmes' tone was one of incredulity.

"Thaf's right, Mr. Holmes," said the willing witness. "The only thing I could think of was that the thief wasn't going to get the other one so I sat up the whole night with my poker just in case he should return. This morning I took the remaining pearl to the Margate Bank and gave it to the manager for safekeeping. Then I got in touch with Mrs. Hudson, whom I knew through the Chelsea Swing Circle, and here I am."

She settled back in her chair with a sense of relief at having told her story.

Knowing Holmes so well, I could sense that the great detective was intrigued, nay fascinated. Most of the cases brought to him, being oft-told tales, produced an air of sympathetic ennui, but such was not the situation now.

"Do I assume," said Holmes, "that you haven't contacted the police regarding this unfortunate occurrence?"

Miss Carstair spread her hands in a gesture of resignation.

"I am not a worldly woman. I wouldn't even know how to go about going to a police station and I fear I would do everything wrong if I did. But I know all about Mr. Sherlock Holmes since I'm an avid reader of the journals. My only thought was that you could guide me in this matter and, of course, recover the missing pearl." Her hands closed about her purse firmly. "My father was a frugal man and when he died I found that he had left me with a sizeable income from Australian bonds at five percent. Naturally, I expect to pay you a fee and I can afford a reasonable one."

Holmes, who detested business, waved this point aside with a rather abrupt gesture.

"The novelty of this matter will serve as my fee for the moment," he said. "I suppose that your idea of what the burglar looks like is on the sketchy side?"

Florence Carstair nodded ruefully. "The only light in the room was from the glowing embers in the fireplace, Mr. Holmes. I've tried my best to recall what happened in those brief moments, but all I can say is that he was average height and, in fact, I couldn't even swear as to whether he wore a mask or not."

"But not overweight," mused Holmes, "and fast on his feet, judging by the speed of his departure."

He thought for a moment as both Miss Carstair and I watched him with eager expectation. Then his manner indicated that he had reached a decision.

"I will investigate this incident, Miss Carstair, but first, I'm going to send a message to Inspector Lestrade at Scotland Yard. I would like you to contact him as soon as you leave here. It will mean telling this whole tale again and he will, no doubt, have numerous questions. Do your best to assist him in whatever way that you can."

Evidently this was not the answer Florence Carstair expected.

"But, sir, why go through all that? If Sherlock Holmes will investigate this strange happening, what need have I of Scotland Yard?"

Holmes' gentle sigh of apparent resignation fooled me not one whit. Actually, the great detective was always delighted at any expression of his invincibility in the field of criminal investigation.

"First, Miss Carstair," he said, "a theft must be reported to the authorities. Second, my dear friend, Dr. Watson, will affirm that my files on all matters pertaining to crime are extensive. However, because of the sheer limitations of space and manpower, they cannot compare with the archives of the Yard. As soon as Lestrade has the prime facts, it will be as though you had fired a boiler under a huge steam engine. The parts will assume motion and the machine will grind into action inexorably and semi-automatically. The man it seeks is agile. Unless he had an accomplice we know nothing about, he is adept at safe-cracking.

You did say that your safe was open, not that it had been blown or jimmied open."

Miss Carstair, her eyes shining with excitement, nodded affirmation of the detective's words.

"This unknown man," Holmes went on, "either knew personally or was informed as to the Carstair pearls and where to find them. The man also entered through your garden. You said that he left via the French windows, which I assume were already open since you did not say that he burst through them." Taking the lady's breathless silence as agreement, he continued. "All of these facts will be fed into the machine and a pattern will begin to emerge: thieves who specialize in gem robberies; thieves who are currently at liberty; thieves who are known to have available sources to dispose of gems as well-known as the black pearls. The machine of Scotland Yard will do a job which I cannot do. And," a smile of possible satisfaction flitted across his face, "this will leave me free to consider the human aspects of the case. The intangibles that machines cannot handle and which are, indeed, the really fascinating aspects of all crime."

Miss Carstair's rather commonplace, broad face was registering puzzlement.

"I can hardly see fascinating intangibles in my problem, Mr. Holmes. The pearls are of great value and were the pride of my father's life. I should have kept them in the bank, I know, but after daddy's passing, I rather left things just as they were. It was his wish they remain in the family should I have any descendants." Here, the common sense of the English middle class produced a rueful smile as she surveyed her considerable bulk. "Since that hardly seems likely, on my death the black pearls are to go to the Tate Museum. Now they've been stolen, or at least one has, and it's as simple as that."

"Your last sentence was the clue, Miss Carstair," said the sleuth. "Robbery is a business and, like most commercial activities, is operated on the principle of profit, the largest profit possible. One-half a robbery is sufficiently novel to fascinate Sherlock Holmes."

With this remark, the great detective rose to his feet indicating that the interview was concluded. Miss Carstair assured him that she would be in touch with Inspector Lestrade post-haste and departed.

Before I could pose a question or even a comment, Holmes rapidly penned a letter which he dispatched via Billy, the page-boy, to Lestrade. Then the great detective leaned back with a satisfied smile on his face and I felt that my moment had arrived.

"I'm inclined to agree with the lady, Holmes," I said. "It does seem like a rather common case to so captivate that imaginative mind of yours."

"I fear you missed a clue, Watson," said Holmes. "However, that could easily be due to the fact that you are not knowledgeable regarding Captain Carstair's fabulous black pearls."
I waited in silence, knowing that Holmes would continue as, of course, he did.

"Where was the thief when Miss Carstair entered the study?" asked Holmes.

"In the room, naturally," I responded, somewhat nettled.

"But not at the safe," stated Holmes. "Miss Carstair said that he was half-way to the French windows and was able to race out of the house so rapidly that she could not tell whether he wore a mask or not. In fact, she really got a very fleeting look at him."

"What is so singular about that?"

"Simply that the thief had opened the safe and then left with only one of the Carstair pearls."

"I disagree, Holmes. The robber could have been at the safe and heard Miss Carstair approaching. He would, naturally, begin his escape before her actual appearance. At least, I would."

"Excellent, my dear Watson. Your reasoning is very sound, but in the field of criminology, it pays to look beyond the obvious. That first though, which seems so apparent, may not be the correct one."

With relish, the detective warmed to his task.

"Picture yourself as the nocturnal intruder," he continued. "You have come to secure the Carstair pearls and are at the safe, which you have succeeded in opening. You hear an approaching footfall. Would you not grab the object of your visit and depart? Would you not take both of the pearls which were together in the safe?"

I was forced to nod in agreement with this logic.

"I reconstruct what happened somewhat differently," Holmes went on. "The thief took one pearl only from the safe. Perhaps he paused in the middle of the room to check on his prize. Then, either he heard Florence Carstair approaching or she just appeared and he bolted. I therefore conclude that he was originally after only one of the black pearls. Does this not seem more than a little *recherche*?"

"Good heavens, Holmes," I sputtered, "now you have me completely confused."

"Some background on the gems in question is called for," replied Holmes. "Being black pearls, and of excellent quality, either of the gems would have a distinct and considerable value. But their real worth lies in being together. These pearls are unique in their field, hence the detailed writing about them by an authority as eminent as Dr. Krenstroff. The Carstair pearls are as close to similar twins as the field of rare gems has ever produced. They have been weighed and measured by the finest Amsterdam experts and are practically identical. This identical aspect is their rare value, for what lady of quality would not toy with the idea of selling her immortal soul to adorn her delicate ears with the two most perfectly matched pearls known. For this reason, the concept of the thief taking just one of these water-born twins presents a puzzle of enormous interest."

"Does it suggest anything, Holmes?"

"Simply that we have an obvious crime with a witness but the motive is obscure. Until we can ferret out the reason for half a robbery, I fear we have a sticky wicket, Watson."

Holmes' misgivings proved well-founded. Lestrade, backed by the files of Scotland Yard, and an army of faceless men grimly bent to their tasks, poured forth suspects. Whereabouts and alibis for the night in question were gone over meticulously. But no hopeful leads developed, nor was there any sign of activity on the part of the possessor of the missing gem. It was as though the entire event had never happened. Holmes combed the byways of the London criminal element in a half dozen of his superb disguises. The Baker Street Irregulars were pressed into service to no avail. The great detective was faced with a case devoid of clues since nothing, absolutely nothing, happened. Finally, Holmes threw up his hands.

"I have nothing to work with. There are no clues or leads. The thief cannot secure the remaining black pearl which is in the vaults of the Margate Bank. There has been no attempt to sell the one pearl in his possession. I am fairly certain of that. We face an impasse, old friend."

On this particular morning, I was working on the conclusion of "The Red Headed League," the first part of which has already been published in the last issue of Strand Magazine. In answer to a question as to my activity, I mentioned this to Holmes, who seemed perplexed.

"This makes no sense, Watson. This recounting of our adventure has already been published and yet you are working on the conclusion?"

"The case history is being presented in two parts, old chap. The publishers trust that my readers, having read the first half of the recounting, will take pains to buy the next issue of the magazine to learn the denouement."

The sleuth gazed at me for a long moment and then clapped his palm to his forehead violently.

"Great heavens, Watson, that's it."

"What is?"

"All along I have assumed that this half a robbery was the first half."

My befuddlement must have been very obvious and Holmes went into more detail, unusual with him, since he oft left me dangling.

"I have been bemused by the fact that the thief could have stolen both pearls but took only one. Suppose this was the second attempt and he actually secured what he was after."

Now Holmes did leave me dangling for there followed a series of events so rapid as to leave me quite breathless. Lestrade was contacted and dispatched to the Margate Bank to secure the pearl left in safe-keeping with the manager. Holmes specifically cautioned Inspector Lestrade to secure the gem immediately and have it taken to the crown jeweler for inspection.

Next, the great detective enlisted the aid of Inspector Gregson. They interviewed the constable whose night-time tour of duty included Horsham Square and the Carstair home. It developed that this dedicated protector of the peace was but recent to his beat, to use an American expression, and had replaced a former policeman now in retirement. With me in tow, Holmes and Gregson located the man in question, one Frederic Frey, whose record with the force was long and excellent. Holmes had taken the trouble to check his newspaper files reaffirming the fact that Captain Carstair had died quietly some fourteen months previously.

Holmes directed his questions to Frey relative to that period when the captain was still living. The former constable had little trouble in providing the information that Holmes was looking for.

"Why, yes, sir. I recollect well an incident like what you describe. Let's see. 'Round two years ago, I'd say. Shortly past midnight I'm on the street and I hears a sound that is suspiciously like a shot. There's lights in the Carstair mansion and I finds Captain Carstair in his garden with a revolver in his hand. He said that he had surprised a robber and got in a shot at him. We went back into his den and he told me that the chap, whoever he was, hadn't had the time to grab anything."

"Do you recall if Captain Carstair's safe was open?" asked Holmes, his eyes glistening.

"No, sir, it wasn't, but the captain checked its contents while I was there." The exconstable's eyes narrowed for a moment in thought. "Now that I recall, he did say something kinda strange-like. I wanted to check out his silver for him but he says: 'No. Whatever he was after would have been in there.' And he indicated the safe. I filed a routine report but frankly I don't place too much faith in attempted robberies." With a quick glance at Inspector Gregson, he continued: "A shadow in the night, an unexplained or strange sound-that part of London gets mighty quiet at that hour. Sometimes it makes people jumpy."

This was all the information Frey had and, indeed, all Holmes seemed interested in.

Upon our return to Scotland Yard, we were met by an excited Inspector Lestrade. He had, at Holmes direction, secured the black pearl from the Margate Bank. The crown jeweler, pressed into rapid service, had pronounced the gem counterfeit but the cleverest reproduction he had ever seen. This startling bit of news did not seem to surprise Holmes a bit. Thanking Lestrade and Gregson for their, as he termed it: "invaluable assistance," the detective dragged me into a hansom cab which he directed to the Diogenes Club with all possible speed.

Bouncing over rough pavement, I finally got a few answers to the many questions plaguing me.

"Suddenly, I realized that the matter of the Black Pearls wasn't one-half a robbery but two, Watson. The thief apprehended by Miss Carstair was only interested in one of the pearls in the safe, the reason being that his employer already had the other one, the other real one, that is. Constable Frey's fortunate confirmation just affirmed a fact that I had already accepted."

Holmes cocked his eye at me to see if I was following this reasoning. Then, with an exhibition of patience rather rare for him, he back-tracked.

"My dear friend, let me unravel this tangled skein from the beginning."

"Please do."

"Around two years ago, a cracksman actually did open the Carstair safe and took one of the Black Pearls, leaving in its place a counterfeit gem. This was the test robbery to see if the ersatz pearl would stand up under the inspection of the owner of the gems. The plan was successful and no robbery was reported. Then recently, Miss Carstair came upon a thief, the same or another, and that is of no consequence, about to do the same thing. He had opened the safe but had to be sure which of the pearls he was after. He took his selection to the only light source available, the embers in the fireplace. At this moment, his presence was discovered and he took off, unable to leave the second counterfeit behind. Had he been able to do so, one of the cleverest robberies in history would have been successful. Two world famous gems purloined and no one the wiser."

By now I was nodding in semi-understanding.

"But why the long period of time between attempts?" I asked.

"Perhaps the false pearls took a long time to create. In any case, the master criminal, being after very big game indeed, was in no hurry. Oh it was a complex web indeed, and only one man could have been the weaver."

"Moriarty," I said, automatically.

"No," replied Holmes, "though the scheme would do credit to his genius. As with most complicated plots, the solution points an unerring finger at its creator. The man we seek has the ability to create a masterful imitation black pearl so perfect as to deceive the real owner of the gem. He also has the standing and reputation to deal with the one type of buyer who could display the black pearls openly but without having them measured or inspected or even suspected. I refer, naturally, to one of the royal houses who could add the black pearls to their crown jewels.

"But Holmes," I exclaimed, "who is at the bottom of this whole affair?"

"Krenstroff, the gem expert. At least that is the theory which I will advance to my brother, Mycroft."

"What connection has Mycroft with this singular robbery?" I was befuddled again.

"Since, in the normal course of things, the Carstair pearls would revert to the Tate Museum, England is involved. The British Secret Service has to enter the picture and Mycroft is the man to pull the strings."

Mycroft Holmes, the second most powerful man in England, caused an event never officially recorded. The vaults of Krenstroff in Berlin were burglarized by what we might assume were a team of imported experts. They found what they were looking for: the true Carstair Black Pearls. They now reside, according to the wishes of that nautical man who originally brought them from the Orient, in the Tate Museum. Inasmuch as one of the royal families of the continent was negotiating with Krenstroff for the purchase of the gems, the entire affair was kept completely secret.

Even Doctor Watson's notes on this event were, at many points, purposely vague. Only the opening of his dispatch box after so many years revealed this unknown case of Sherlock Holmes.

THE POISON PLOT

It was mid-morning on a weekday and my intimate friend, the world's only consulting detective, and I were just finishing a late breakfast. Outside it was clear but cold as a north wind drove over England pushing cirrus clouds from horizon to horizon. The rays of a winter sun limped earthward bringing light but little heat. Passers-by on Baker Street were buried in coat collars and barricaded behind mufflers. Those without gloves had their hands dug deeply into pockets.

I was diligently applying some of Mrs. Hudson's home-made marmalade to a last popover with glances at the "Morning Banner" as I did so. Holmes, between sips of coffee, was going over notes he had made relative to a mysterious murder committed on the Continent, possibly with the thought that he would be consulted about it.

The tranquil atmosphere was intruded upon by a rap on the door. At a word from Holmes, Mrs. Hudson appeared in the outer portal of the famous suite of rooms the sleuth and I shared.

"A Doctor Digbody to see you, sir," she said.

"Fancy that," replied Holmes. "Do show him up, Mrs. Hudson, and my thanks." As our landlady vanished, he turned to me. "You remember, Digbody?"

As I shook my head, he continued. "Oh, perhaps your paths have not crossed. General practice, relatively successful, and the good man has a genius for analysis. He has been helpful to me on several occasions. I did once suggest that he change his name. Digbody...hmmmm...hardly appropriate for one in medicine, would you say?"

My thoughts on the subject were suppressed as the subject of our discussion arrived. As Holmes assisted our visitor out of his coat, I noted that Digbody was fairly tall and very neat and tidy in appearance, though his ample shock of hair was somewhat windblown. His long hands, while carefully tended, revealed chemical stains much in the same manner that Holmes' did. As Digbody unwound a white silk muffler, introductions were made and, after mouthing the usual greetings to my fellow member of the medical profession, I got him seated in our Queen Anne chair. Holmes then made an observation.

"You are an early bird, Digbody, on this most inclement day. I see that you are but recently from the suburbs but took the time to drop by your flat before your arrival here."

Digbody's eyes widened with that surprised look, so common to visitors of Sherlock Holmes, as was the expression of puzzlement which replaced it.

"I have just come from Kensington," he stated, "and did drop by my digs for a moment, though I'm blessed if I know how you figured that."

"Your clogs," said Holmes, indicating the doctor's serviceable galoshes, "have been in recent contact with the snow. I rather imagine that some has fallen in the outskirts. And those unopened envelopes in your suit coat pocket, they must have come by late post. Simple observation indicates that you came from the suburbs but went to your lodgings for your mail. Of course, deduction reinforces the later proposition."

"How?" asked Digbody. He was no waster of words.

"Your scarf, my dear chap. Much more suited to formal evening wear. I imagine the north wind prompted you to grab the first one at hand, probably on your way out of your flat."

As Digbody shook his head in wonderment, I joined the conversation. "Holmes has an extraordinary genius for minutiae," I remarked.

"As I well know," agreed Digbody. "Actually, that's why I'm here." His eyes centered on Holmes apologetically. "This problem arose in connection with my practice and I could only think of you. I do hope my visit is not inopportune."

"Of course not," replied Holmes with gusto. "Since Watson and I have no intention of braving the elements, what better thing than a problem to consider and solve. Do tell us all," concluded the detective as I nodded with eager anticipation.

"I may be sitting on top of an attempted murder," was Digbody's melodramatic response. "That's the nuts and bolts of it."

Once started, his words tumbled forth.

"I was called in on a case at the insistence of the patient, one Montgomery Vail. The chap recently retired from the foreign service and lives in a gloomy, barn-like house out in Kensington. Mrs. Vail is a rather quiet woman, sort of fades into the surroundings, you know."

"Self-effacing," commented Holmes. "Frequently an asset in the diplomatic corps." Noting my escalating eyebrows, he added, by way of explanation: "Other wives are not jealous of her, you see."

"To be sure," continued Digbody, as I nodded in understanding. "I was a bit bothered about medical ethics but the Vail's family doctor seemed happy to wash his hands of the whole thing.

He had diagnosed Vail as suffering from influenza. With complications," he added, with a quick half-smile at me.

"The addition meaning 'I don't know'," I said drily.

"Exactly," said Digbody. "After a superficial examination, I saw no reason to disagree. There is an epidemic of influenza in France now and quite a few cases on this side of the channel as well. I was writing out a prescription for the poor fellow and at that moment we were alone in his bedroom. Vail seemed ro rouse himself from a semi-coma. 'Doctor Digbody,' he said, 'you have a considerable reputation as an analyst. I want you to know that I am being poisoned.'"

"I was thunderstruck, naturally. My patient's words seemed to exhaust him and he sank back into his pillow and a restless sleep. I really didn't know quite what to do."

"A most uncomfortable situation," I murmured in sympathy.

"My first thought," continued Digbody, "was the obvious and easy one. Vail was in delirium which might explain his remarkable statement. Then it occurred to me that his symptoms could indicate poisoning. Mrs. Vail was still downstairs securing the milk toast I had suggested, so I popped into Vail's bathroom and found his comb and brush. It took but a moment to get several strands of his hair into an envelope. I was sitting by the patient when Mrs. Vail returned."

"Capital!" said Holmes, with enthusiasm. "You might try the field of detection if you ever weary of medicine."

Digbody's face flushed with pleasure. "I'll leave that in your capable hands, Holmes."

"Of course you analyzed the hair samples?"
Digbody nodded. "Arsenic. And it was present in the hair ends." He addressed me. "Don't you agree, Doctor, that the poison must have been introduced some time ago to have gotten that far?"

My reply was somewhat tentative. "Yes, I would think so."

"About a month," stated Holmes. "The whole thing bears a resemblance to a case in Venice a decade ago. A wife introduced, at intervals, arsenic into her husband's food. In very small amounts at first. Since her husband's resultant illness was gradual, poison was not suspected."

"Was she successful? The wife, I mean?"

"In part, Watson," responded Holmes. "The husband died. However, he was a chemist and, unknown to his wife, had donated his body to science. A doctor detected the arsenic in the liver and intestines of the corpse. A very ingenious murder was thus exposed."

"Do you think, Holmes, that this case could be similar?" Digbody's face was stern.

"Possibly. The more so if one of Vail's tours of duty took the husband and wife to Italy. But let us not jump to conclusions."

Holmes rose to his feet and began pacing the room with that quick, nervous stride that I knew so well.

"How many servants in the Vail household?" he asked.

"Three. Before I left, I made sure that Mrs. Vail and the servants understood that the master of the house was to have nothing to eat until I returned."

"Very good thinking, Digbody."

"Indeed," I echoed. "With a new doctor on the case, the murderer might want to hurry the job."

"I believe Vail is safe enough for the moment. He is very weak, of course, but there probably isn't more than a grain of arsenic in his body now. Not a fatal amount, but..." Digbody's words dwindled to a halt.

"But," said Sherlock Holmes, "the stage is set. The coup d'etat is a near thing. It would seem to me, gentlemen, that some haste on all our parts is required."

It was arranged that Doctor Digbody would return to Kensington immediately. Holmes assured him that we would be on his heels.

Following his departure, Holmes and I dressed warmly and did brave the elements after all.

Upon our arrival in the London suburb, Holmes showed

no interest in the Vail mansion but directed his footsteps towards the local pharmacy. As we entered the establishment, he broke his thoughtful silence.

"You know, Watson, poison is a subtle weapon, but it does narrow the field."

"You mean the culprit must be in regular contact with the victim."

"Exactly," said Holmes, with a pleased expression. "I think we can concentrate on the actual members of the Vail household. For the time being, at least."

"It can't be. Yes, it is. Mr. Sherlock Holmes!"

The pharmacy appeared deserted and momentarily we could not locate the source of the loud voice that rang out. As we exchanged startled glances, there was the sound of movement from the rear of the establishment and a youngish man rushed from behind the drug counter towards us.

"And surely this is the good Doctor Watson," continued the sandy-haired man as he descended upon us and energetically pumped Holmes' hand. "Just wait until my dear mater hears of this."

I sputtered an uncomfortable: "Awfully sorry, can't seem..." but got no further.

"Oh dear, you don't know me. Probably never would without chance bringing you here." He peered into Holmes' hawk-like face with a half-amazed, half-reverent expression.

"I'm Cooldock, gentlemen, Horace Cooldock. Chief pharmacist here. Only one, in fact. When I studied for the trade, my good old professor was a great admirer of your medico-legal discoveries, Mr. Holmes. Especially your hemoglobin precipitate re-agent for the testing of blood stains (see *"A Study in Scarlet"*). No doubt Doctor Watson was of some help in that discovery."

"Actually, no," said Holmes, recovering somewhat from the enthusiastic greeting. "I chanced upon that process at the time that Watson and I were originally introduced."

"Well, it certainly made the gualacum test old hat," continued the pharmacist. He turned to me and insisted on shaking my hand. "How indebted I am to you, sir, for your recounting of Mr. Holmes adventures. Needless to say, I have read and re-read every one."

Holmes directed a frosty glance in my direction. Ever since his brother, Mycroft Holmes, had said in Holmes presence: "I hear of Sherlock everywhere since you became his chronicler" (see *"The Greek Interpreter"*), the great detective had blamed me for making him a figure of sensationalism. This bothered me not a whit since I knew that Holmes secretly was delighted by the aura of infallibility which surrounded his name.

Horace Cooldock bubbled on. "You gentlemen are not here without a reason. How can I be of help?" He directed a conspiratorial glance towards us. "Mum's the word and all that."

Seldom had Holmes been blessed with such an eager witness.

"I do have a small interest," stated the detective, "in the household of Montgomery Vail. Are you familiar with anyone there?"

"Indeed I am. New to the area, you see. Bound to notice them."

"Have they made any purchases here?" inquired the detective.

Cooldock was on familiar ground. "Indeed they have, sir. I've filled a number of prescriptions for the gentleman who, I understand, has been a bit under the weather since they arrived."

Holmes' keen glance sparked an answer to an unspoken question.

"No sir, I haven't ever seen Mr. Vail. The butler has been in several times. Mrs. Vail, also, for household supplies. Quite a gardener, Mrs. Vail."

"How do you know that?" queried Holmes.

"Bought some arsenic, she did. Fairly large amount. Uses it for a spray on the flowers to kill mealy worms. The mater is keen on that sort of thing. Mentioned it to her and she said it would work."

Holmes had learned what he wanted but he asked several more general questions to divert his eager ally. Then we departed but not before Horace Cooldock had given me his name and address and extracted a promise that I would write him as soon as I had another case history ready for publication.

On the quiet street outside, I was the one who waxed enthusiastic. "I say, Holmes, we struck a rich vein there."

"So rich," said the sleuth, "that I believe we are now ready to visit the actual scene of these strange doings."

Following directions received from Doctor Digbody, Holmes set a brisk pace for the Vail abode.

In the gloomy Tudor mansion set well back from the road, Digbody introduced us to Mrs. Vail. Digbody's patient was upstairs in a fitful sleep. The servants were all in the rear of the house. We were in the sizeable drawing room and a look of alarm crossed the face of the lady when she heard the name of Sherlock Holmes.

"But, Mr. Holmes, you are a detective. What brings you to these parts?"

"An unofficial consulting detective," replied Holmes, automatically. He was always didactic about titles. "However, I do dabble in forensic medicine, Mrs. Vail. Poisons in particular and it was on this subject that Doctor Digbody consulted with me."

"Poisons?" Mrs. Vail's hand adjusted a strand of her dark hair. She was younger than I had pictured her. Her pale face, though drawn and worn from worry, had a firm bone structure.

After a long look into Holmes' eyes, Mrs. Vail continued: "Would you please explain?"

"You are evidently a dedicated gardener, Mrs. Vail," said Holmes. "I deduced that from the state of the flower beds outside."

An expression of pleasure flitted across Lenore Vail's face.

"The place was rather overgrown when we first came."

"A situation which you have obviously remedied. Now, Mrs. Vail, do you by any chance use an arsenic spray on your flowers?"

"Yes," she responded.

"And most effective it is, too," continued Holmes. "Do not be alarmed, but there is little doubt that your husband is suffering from arsenic poisoning." Holmes rode over the gasp of dismay from the lady. "It is quite possible that your husband has a very low tolerance for this poison. An errant breeze, some of the spray wafted through an open window, might cause your husband to react in a most unusual manner."

"Good heavens!" said Mrs. Vail. "I have done a lot of spraying. But I never dreamed it could be the cause of Montgomery's illness."

Both Digbody and I had a problem concealing our amazement. Holmes' words had no basis in fact whatsoever. "He is laying a false scent," I thought. "Obviously the lady knows nothing of poisons or, if she does, she must consider Holmes a fool."

"Mrs. Vail, perhaps we can dispense with the flower spray for a while."

Lenore's voice was vehement. "I'll never use the terrible stuff again."

Holmes' raised palm stemmed further words.

"At the moment, this thought is just a working hypothesis." He directed his eyes to Digbody. "Perhaps Doctor Watson and I could see your patient. With the permission of Mrs. Vail, naturally."

The lady rose. "Of course, Mr. Holmes. Anything to have Montgomery well again."

She led the way towards the great stairway in the entrance hall. At the foot of the stairs, Holmes paused to gaze admiringly at a life-size oil on the wall. It depicted Lenore Vail in her late teens in a formal gown. Her high cheekbones and the shadow they cast were strongly defined by the artist.

"The infant prodigy," said Holmes cryptically.

"Millais," added Digbody.

"My uncle commissioned the painting," said Mrs. Vail simply.

It was my thought that the years had been kind to the

lady. One could never doubt that the painting was of her or that, in more exciting and colorful surroundings, she would be extraordinarily pleasing in appearance.

As we mounted the stairs, I wondered what a painting of the renowned John Everett Millais was doing in the home of a government employee of scant fame. His works certainly fetch a fine fee, nowadays, I thought.

(Note: It is interesting to consider that Watson's comment could indicate that Millais was alive at the time of this happening. This would place the date of the adventure no later than 1896.)

The bedroom of the patient was dark. A single gas jet threw a feeble light on the scene and permitted obscure shadows in the corners of the large room. One wall had a recessed area of about eight feet which, at one time, might have been the haven for a breakfront or armoire. In it now was an old-fashioned bed hung with silk-lined tapestry. Directly opposite the bed, which seemed to protrude from the wall, was a row of windows which were heavily curtained. As Mrs. Vail entered and indicated for the others to follow, a figure in the bed stirred. Montgomery Vail was a corpulent man, if the outline of his blankets was to be believed. Drawing closer, I noted that his face was obese and flaccid with a pasty hue. As Lenore Vail arrived at the side of the bed available for traffic, a loose floorboard squeaked loudly and suddenly. The sound reached the man in the bed and one eye fluttered open, then the other. His mouth opened several times and then he managed words in a voice hoarse with weakness.

"I seem to have attracted a delegation." As his eyes rested on Holmes, his thin lips parted in a humorless smile. "Surely this gentleman is a mortician."

A thin cackle forced its way up from his chest with a chilling sound. For one of the very few times in my memory, Holmes seemed non-plussed. He had frequently been referred to, usually by the lawless, as a figure of doom but never as the attendant after death.

As Mrs. Vail placed a cool hand on her husband's forehead, Digbody reassured his patient. "Dr. Watson and an associate were in the neighborhood. I asked them to have a look at you."

As I automatically took Vail's wrist, feeling for the pulse, it occurred to me that the sick man bore a resemblance to a buddha, though there was no oriental cast to his face. An apparently unrelated thought crossed my mind as I realized suddenly that Mrs. Vail did have a semi-oriental quality to her features. The pulse under my fingers was stronger than I had anticipated.

"It's a bad sign when doctors congregate," muttered Vail.

"Now, now..." Digbody's tone was brisk. "Additional opinions can sometimes be most helpful." He glanced towards me. "However, I am sure that Dr. Watson concurs with me. Despite what you think, I'm sure this is nothing more than a seious case of influenza."

I nodded. It seemed the thing to do. Holmes had remained in the background, studying the figure in the large bed. After fluffing her husband's pillows, Mrs. Vail joined Holmes. Digbody and I exchanged a few comments more noteworthy for their technical sound than any information they contained.

"I believe I'll have some beef bouillon prepared for you," said Digbody as he crossed towards the door. When I vacated the bedside to join him, I heard the floor squeak again. Downstairs, Mrs. Vail went to the kitchen to prepare the bouillon. Holmes accompanied her to have a few words with the servants. When he reappered with Lenore Vail, it was the detective who was carrying the tray with the bowl of clear broth and plate of plain biscuits.

"Excellent beef broth," he stated. "I had a spoonful myself. Now I'll take this up to your husband, Mrs. Vail. Perhaps there is something which Watson or Digbody wish to say to you."

Without waiting for a reply, the detective went up the stairs quickly.

Lenore Vail watched his retreating figure for a moment and then turned to Digbody. "Doctor, upstairs you mentioned influenza again. But Mr. Holmes said that Montgomery was suffering from arsenic poisoning."

"Poison is an alarming word," was his reply. "In your husband's present condition, let us try to keep him from any worries."

I was surprised to hear the bedroom floorboard creak and automatically placed Holmes at the patient's bedside. "It is an old house," I thought. "Evidently sound travels in it."

"I don't want you fretting either, Mrs. Vail," continued Digbody. "We shall pull your husband through. Meanwhile, I am a trifle concerned about you."

A single sounding of the door chimes interrupted him. The butler appeared quickly from the rear of the house, opened the door and picked up the evening paper from the veranda.

"No matter how ill he is, Montgomery insists on looking at the journals morning and night. When he was still active, we traveled a great deal. A newspaper from home was a thing to treasure."

Digbody recaptured his interrupted thought as the butler mounted the stairs, paper in hand.

"You have been under a considerable strain, Mrs. Vail. My prescription for you is some overdue sleep." As the lady began to form an objection, he continued: "I will arrange this evening for a nurse to be here bright and early tomorrow morning. She need stay for only a few days and her presence is as much for your sake as your husband's." Digbody's manner was firm. "I shall wait for a little while and then check your husband's condition before departure. The butler can let me out. Now I see no reason why you should not retire immediately, Mrs. Vail. You can be of scant use to your ailing husband if you are not in good health yourself."

Lenore Vail had no answer to this statement and curbed her hostess manner in the face of it. Holmes and the butler appeared on the upper landing as she was saying her goodnights. After a pleasant word or two with Holmes and some instructions to the butler, she disappeared into her own room on the opposite side of the stairwell from her husband's.

Alone in the great hail, we stared at each other.

"Have you learned anything, Holmes?" I queried.

"Quite a lot," stated Holmes. "And none of it helpful to the devoted wife. I want to have just a word with the gardener and then we'd better be back to Baker Street."

As Holmes retired to the servant's quarters, Digbody went upstairs to check his patient's condition. The two men returned at the same time. Digbody reported that Montgomery Vail seemed somewhat improved. Holmes had little to say until we were on our way back to the metropolitan center.

'There are many times that I recoil at what seems overly obvious," he confided, "but one cannot deny the existence of facts. Fact: Montgomery Vail is suffering from chronic arsenic poisoning. Fact: Lenore Vail purchased a large amount of arsenic from the local pharmacy. Fact: Mrs. Vail does all the cooking. The servants consist of the butler, a housemaid, and a gardener. Evidently, Vail approves of his wife's activities in the kitchen since he did not choose to secure a cook. Fact: The gardener, when I questioned him, did admit that Mrs. Vail used more arsenic in her spray than he would have considered necessary. Fact: Lenore Vail prepared the spray herself."

"The net seems to be tightening around the lady. But how about the motive?" I had not been with Holmes for so long without developing some instincts regarding detection.

"I can give you one," replied Holmes, "though it does not charm me. Lenore Vail is considerably younger than her husband though she does little for her appearance. In fact, the pains she takes to appear plain are unusual and therefore suspicious. Vail, on the other hand, has slipped badly. His appearance is hardly appealing and I rather imagine his career with the foreign office was disappointing. What has Lenore to look forward to but a dull life with a retired and rapidly aging husband?"

"But what are we to do?" asked Digbody.

"If we accept Lenore Vail as the guilty party, the fact that we know her husband is suffering from arsenic poisoning, plus my appearance on the scene, will prevent her from continuing with the scheme. She did not strike me as being a foolish woman."

And so the matter stood until the following morning.

Sleep came hard to me that night. The cold aggravated my old wound received in the fatal battle of Maiwand. The pain subsided in the early morning hours, allowing me to fall into an exhausted sleep. As a consequence, I was late in rising and found Holmes missing.

I was consoling myself with a second large kipper when Holmes returned to our lodgings. The detective seemed especially alert and his eyes held, again, the sparkle of the chase. Somewhat grumpily I registered a complaint.

"Really, Holmes, you allow me to remain abed while you are out having all the fun."

"The fun," said the detective with a chuckle, "consisted in going over dusty files at the Yard. I had exhausted my own clippings by eight a.m."

"What were you looking into?"

"The past, which is so often the key to the future. I also dropped by the foreign office and completed my morning jaunt in Harley Street."

"Oh?" I said, hoping for more news.

"One Harriet Ness, a practical nurse and a policewoman as well, is now down in Kensington tending to Montgomery Vail. It is Miss Ness who will prepare the food for the ailing man at the doctor's orders."

"That should spike any poisoning attempts."

"One would think so," responded Holmes. "We will drop by later in the day and see what fate has dealt us in this affair." A faraway look came to the detective's eyes. "I have a most uncomfortable feeling. This case could end in a stalemate like the cursed Windbank affair."(3)

Our journey to Kensington came sooner than planned since, before noon, our page boy brought Holmes a cable. As he read it, Holmes' lips tightened and his penetrating eyes swiveled towards me. "We leave immediately, old fellow, the game's afoot."

Outside, Holmes handed me the message. It read: "Montgomery Vail just died from a cause you might anticipate. Digbody."

"I say, Holmes," I said excitedly, "what strange farrago is this?"

Holmes' eyes were thoughtful. "When everything else proves impossible, what seems impossible must be true."

Having repeated a pet idea, the great detective lapsed into silence as we made our way to Kensington.

Inside the gloomy suburban mansion of the late Montgomery Vail, we found Doctor Digbody awaiting our arrival. With him was a most capable-looking woman with a "no nonsense" air about her. Holmes evidently knew her, addressing her as Miss Ness.

"The policewoman," I thought.

Digbody briefed us rapidly. "I checked the patient when I arrived. The bed-clothes were in a considerable disarray as though he had suffered a seizure. He was dead. I can tell you now what the autopsy will prove. Death by arsenic poisoning."

"That is impossible, Doctor," said Harriet Ness. Her voice was calm but did not lack in authority.

"One moment," interrupted Holmes. "Where is Mrs. Vail?"

"In her room," replied Digbody. "She took the terrible news quite well but was obviously close to hysteria. I felt it wise to give her a sedative and insist that she lie down. The drug has taken effect so it won't be possible to question her now."

"Nor is it necessary," said Holmes. His eyes returned to the policewoman. "What was your point, Miss Ness?"

"When I arrived this morning, the patient was in relatively good condition. I prepared the breakfast according to Dr. Digbody's instructions. I was present when the patient ate it. Since that time, no one else was in the room until Dr. Digbody arrived."

"When was the last time you saw Vail?" asked Holmes.

"When I took the paper to him. It was delivered late today." Her brows knitted for a moment. "I also filled his water carafe from the tap in his bedroom. When I left, he was reading the paper with great interest."

I could not restrain myself. "But this is impossible. What could have happened?"

"I know what happened," stated Holmes, "and I believe I know why."

He rose from a large armchair and crossed the hall to gaze at the Millais painting which seemed to interest him so much. Suddenly, he turned to Harriet Ness. "Would you get me the newspaper you took to the deceased?"

"Of course, Mr. Holmes." She went rapidly up the stairs.

"I don't mean to keep you in suspense, gentlemen," continued Holmes. "While Miss Ness secures what I suspect will be the final clue in what Watson referred to as 'a strange farrago', let us consider our facts. There is no doubt that Vail was being slowly poisoned by arsenic. It is obvious that his wife had the means and opportunity to administer the poison. It is also apparent that she alone was a suspect. The servants had no reasons whatsoever and any enemies that Vail might have had could not have reached him. Now let me introduce what may seem to be an unrelated fact, though I believe it had much to do with what occurred."

Holmes crossed to the painting again, indicating it to Digbody and me.

"Here we have a life-size oil by Millais, a painter of international repute. So famous, in fact, that he was made baronet by the queen. Surely this painting must have been costly. Far too costly for a man in Vail's financial state. His wife explained this simply by mentioning that her uncle had commissioned the painting. I made little note of the remark at the time but it came back to haunt me. As did the subject of the painting. Consider the face, gentlemen, and especially the high cheekbones."

"Like a Cossack," I muttered.

"You are close, Watson. The Magyars. Another race of horsemen who invaded and settled in Austria-Hungary. The Magyar cheekbone is as distinctive a feature as the Hapsburg lip, so evident in any painting of Anne of Austria."

Harriet Ness descended the stairs with the newspaper which Holmes had requested. The detective's eyes devoured the front page and a smile of satisfaction altered his stern features.

"Let me read this to you: 'Earl of Broom dies in family castle after long illness'."

He placed the paper on an occasional table.

Digbody was puzzled. "Is that headline revealing?"

Holmes nodded. "It is, when you remember that the house of Broom is a very famous one. The males of the family were invariably in the military. As was often the case in olden times, England was frequently ruled by enemies of this ancient family. On such occasions, the Broom men sought employment in foreign armies. Two of them were hired by the Hapsburgs and achieved great prominence in the Austrian Army. They married in the land of their employment and brought foreign wives back to England when the political climate was more suitable for their presence. Thus the Magyar strain was introduced into this old Saxon blood line."

A realization came to me. "You learned that Mrs. Vail is a Broom?"

"Indeed I did, Watson. I imagine that the now departed Earl of Broom was responsible for this Millais painting. And that Mrs. Vail will now come into a considerable sum of money, having survived her uncle."

I shook my head in a discouraged fashion. "Your analysis is masterful and fascinating, Holmes, but how does it tie in with Vail's death?"

"In the original plot, Montgomery Vail was not supposed to die. You will note that the Earl of Broom was in the throes of a long illness. Being very old, indeed, it was just a matter of time. Vail, anticipating that his wife would become an heiress of note, used the time to his advantage. He poisoned himself."

"Oh come now, Holmes." Doctor Digbody was not convinced.

"Wait," said the detective. "Vail took small doses of arsenic for two reasons. First, his sickness had to cast strong suspicion upon his wife. Second, after a month's time, Vail's body would have a semi-immunity to the poison. A dosage which would kill a nor-

mal person would only render him severely ill because of this
induced tolerance. The time table of the plot was based on the
Earl of Broom's death. Following this, Vail intended to apparently recover. At a suitable time, he would dine with Mrs. Vail,
making sure the dishes they both ate were poisoned. She would
die and he would recover. The entire incident would be passed
off as a miscalculation on the part of Mrs. Vail."

Digbody was convinced now. "How macabre!" he said,
with a shudder.

"But Holmes, what alerted you to this most intricate
scheme? And why did Vail die?"

"The first question, Watson, is so obvious that I shall answer the second one first. Vail was playing a dangerous game
with a weapon he did not understand. The newspaper gave him
the information he had been waiting for. He was ready to progress
to the final act of his carefully-planned drama. He took a last
dosage of arsenic to increase his tolerance and overdid it. He
died by his own hand. As to my unmasking Montgomery Vail as
the true culprit, we have Miss Ness to thank for that. She was the
last one to see Vail alive. She kept a constant vigil on his room
and until you, Digbody, arrived, no one went into that room. No
one else had the opportunity to poison Vail so the seemingly impossible had to be true. Vail was poisoning himself. Once I arrived at this conclusion, the other threads quickly wove the fab-
ric we call motive."

"It's tight," admitted Digbody. "I just hope you can prove
it."

"Of course," said Holmes, as he directed his attention to
Miss Ness. "While you kept watch on the victim's door, did you
hear anything?"

"You mean that squeaky floorboard right by the bed?"

"She's sharp," I thought as Holmes nodded.

"No, Mr. Holmes. I didn't hear a sound."

"Good," said Holmes. "That means that Vail did not leave
his bed. Therefore the arsenic which he used must have been
secreted in the bed itself."

It was. An ornament on a bedpost was loose. In the cavity under it was a packet of arsenic crystals, the weapon used by the murderer. How fortunate that his victim was himself.

Thus ended one of the strangest cases in Holmes' long career. There was nothing to be gained by exposing the villainy of Montgomery Vail so the whole matter was suppressed.

Footnotes of Watson reveal that there was one other result from what he chose to call *"The Poison Plot."* Doctor Digbody was most grateful to Holmes for extricating him from a very touchy situation. To prove it, he agreed to a request of the great detective and had his solicitor apply for a change of name. After a suitable period of time, Hubert "Goodbody," M.D. had to move into much larger quarters on Harley Street to accommodate his rapidly-growing practice.

* * * * *

Footnotes:

1: Because of the prominence of those involved, this baffling case was kept secret for many years. It was only after Holmes retired from London and was engaged in bee-farming on the Sussex Downs, that Watson released a carefully-guarded account of the incident to the public.

2: The fact that Watson was immediately familiar with Mendel indicates that this adventure must have taken place around 1900. Mendel's law was made public in 1865 and generally ignored by biologists. At the turn of the century, however, three of the leading biologists of the day concurred with Mendel's finding and they became the basis of the modern scientific theory of heredity.

3: See "A Case of Identity." It is interesting to note that this adventure, in which James Windibank never paid the piper for his cruel deceit, remained a cockleburr under Holmes' saddle blanket for many years.

About the Author:

Frank Thomas has written many books dealing with the immortal sleuth, Sherelock Holmes. This is his 11th Holmees book. Since his works have been published in America, England, Germany, Israel and Russia, he must be the world's most widely read post-Doyle author.

Prior to fiction writing, he enjoyed an illustrous performing career. He was and is the leading child performer in the history of the Broadway theatre. This led to feature or starring roles in 15 major studio films, innemerable radio shows and finally he starred as the lead in "Tom Corbett, Space Cadet" on national TV for five years in the 1950s.

He is single, resides in Hollywood, chases girls, and plays a very bad game of gold.

REFERENCE MATERIAL FOR THE COLLECTABLE PAPERBACK HOBBY

all the items in this flyer are published by me, or imported by me, and are available for sale from me at:

Gryphon Publications
PO Box 209
Brooklyn, NY 11228-0209
U.S.A.

Please include $2 p/h with each order and allow 3-4 weeks for delivery.

PAPERBACK PARADE: The Magazine for Paperback Readers and Collectors is my own magazine and is the longest-running and leading magazine in the hobby. Each issue is crammed full of cover reproductions of rare books, news, articles, interviews, book lists, ads and more! Published bi-monthly, with 100+ pages, digest, color cover, it covers ALL aspects of the hobby world-wide! Send SASE for a complete list of the highlights of our 50 back issues! Almost all are in stock! All issues are $7 ($8 outside USA); 6-issue Subscription: $35; (outside USA by surface mail, $42).

PAPERBACK, PULP and COMIC COLLECTOR: early 90s UK import stapled mag, concentrates on UK paperbacks, pulps & comics, about 100 pages each, full of excellent material and many covers. Issues #1-8 in stock available $7 each. Special set of all 8 issues for $50ppd in USA.

PAPERBACK AND PULP COLLECTOR: a new, improved version of above, a 120pp trade pb, with color covers, UK import, full of fascinating articles on US and UK pbs and pulps with many covers shown. Issues #1-4 available @ $12 each. Special set of all 4 issues for $45ppd USA.

AUSTRALIAN VINTAGE PAPERBACK GUIDE by Graeme Flanagan, a huge Gryphon book that lists almost all Aust. pbs, much rare info never before revealed, not a price guide, but a guide to these scarce books and their publishers. Trade paperback, 200+ pages, Color Cover and insert. Available in D/J PB ed @ $20; Limited Hardcover D/J ed @ $30.

THE MUSHROOM JUNGLE, a history of Postwar UK paperback publishing, by Steve Holland, stunning UK import, 200pp, Color cover and inside, many great UK pbs cover reporos, a great book, copies available @ $25.

DIFFICULT LIVES by James Sallis, Full-color dust-jacketed Gryphon trade paperback exploring the work of these 3 hardboiled pb writers: Jim Thompson, Chester Himes and David Goodis. Excellent. Available @ $15

RAYMOND CHANDLER AND DASHIELL HAMMETT IN PAPERBACK by Gary Lovisi, Gryphon trade-pb in full-color D/J, lists all US and many foreign vintage pbs, with a hundred covers shown, available @ $15.

DOUBLE YOUR PLEASURE: The Ace Science Fiction Double by James A. Corrick, lists all books in this great series with notes and history, $6.95

PULPS INTO PAPERBACKS by Roy G. James, Gryphon trade pb, full-color D/J listing most of the pulp mag heroes that have been translated into paperback books, profusely illustrated, available @ $15.

NOVEL LIBRARY: Paperback Parade Collector Special #1 by Gary Lovisi, new, on this series of sexy, early sleaze, bibliography, history, and examination with covers of every book shown in color, available @ $15.

BRITISH GANGSTER AND EXPLIOTATION PAPERBACKS by Maurice Flanagan, a stunning UK import, with info and many great covers on these hardboiled, good-girl, highly collected gangster digests, available @ $15

VULTURES OF THE VOID by Phil Harbottle and Steve Holland, Borgo trade-pb, excellent history of the 50s UK SF pb scene, available @ $20.

THE MOVIE TIE-IN BOOK by Moe Wadle, Nostalgia Press book that covers all these great and increasingly collected pbs, a must-have item, with many covers shown and some prices, available @ $20.

PAPERBACKS AUCTION by Gorgon Books, a compiling of all pb auction results from 1991-1995, listing thousands of prices actually paid for collectable pbs, nearest thing there is to an updated PB guide, large trade-pb full of valuable info, available @ $15.

DENNIS McLAUGHLIN: MASTER OF LIGHT AND SHADE by Francis Hertzberg, Gryphon book on this excellent UK artist, his work, concentrating on his pb covers, and history, Full-color D/J and color insert in both states: Trade PB @ $20; Limited/Signed/Numbered Hardcover @ $40.

SCIENCE FICTION DETECTIVE TALES by Gary Lovisi, early pb collector reference deals with all SF-detective books in pb, available @ $7.95

PULPMASTERS by James Van Hise, fine Pulp mag history that is full of great articles and artwork, many pulp covers shown, available @ $20.

PULP HEROES OF THE 30s, by James Van Hise, similar to above, concentrates on the great heroes, Spider, Doc, Shadow, and many others with fine articles, much interior and cover art shown, available @ $20.

AMAZING PULP HEROES by Link Hullar and Frank Hamilton, expansion of book on all the pulp heroes featuring fine written material by pulp scholar Hullar and a hundred+ incredible Frank Hamilton illustrations, 200pp trade-pb in full-color DJ: PB @ $20; Limited Signed/Numbered TPB @ $25.

A GUIDE THROUGH THE WORLDS OF ROBERT A. HEINLEIN by J. Lincoln Thorner, excellent study of author and his work, available @ $6.95

GRYPHON PUBLICATIONS
PO BOX 209, BROOKLYN, NY 11228-0209, USA